Mail Order Mommy
A Brides of Beckham Story
Kirsten Osbourne

Chapter One

BERNIECE JOHNSON SAT in Josephine's Café in Beckham, Massachusetts, trying to force herself to smile at the man her parents had chosen for her to marry, Albert Chase. Mr. Chase had been her father's boss for as long as she could remember, but the truth was, he was not a pleasant man. Not at all.

"So, your mother tells me that she has employed a seamstress to make you the perfect dress and a trousseau. I adore the color red, so you must be certain that all of your bed clothes are in crimson." Albert smiled at her, and it made her stomach roll. She couldn't imagine going to bed with the man. He was older than her father.

"Don't you think it would be better for you if you found a woman . . . closer to your age?" Berniece asked in a whisper. She knew it would offend him, but if she was careful, perhaps he would break their engagement, and she could still have a good relationship with her parents. She dearly wanted them to be happy with her, even though they'd arranged a marriage for her with this odious man.

He frowned. "A woman my age would be past her childbearing years, wouldn't she? Are you trying to deprive me of children?"

"No, sir. Of course not. But I'm only nineteen. I cannot imagine you want to be married to a woman who is young enough to be your daughter." *Or granddaughter.* Berniece kept her voice soft, hoping he would find the words less scathing if she didn't speak them loudly.

"You will be punished for those words on our wedding night," he said calmly as he brought his water to his lips. "You need to learn that you cannot talk to your husband that way." His eyes looked positively gleeful that he would have an excuse to "punish" her, and it made her feel sick all over again. He was not a man any reasonable woman would have chosen for her husband, and she couldn't marry him, but she also couldn't disobey her parents.

"I was just suggesting you might be happier with someone else." Berniece was desperately afraid of this man. She couldn't tell what was going through his mind. But whatever it was, it frightened her, and she didn't want to be part of a marriage to him. She didn't want to have to look at him.

"Haven't you ever been taught that you shouldn't speak every little thought that pops into your head?" A slow smile crossed his face. "I'm sure I'll enjoy teaching you that."

A shudder ripped through her. She couldn't marry this man. Anything would be preferable to a life tied to him. Anything. "I'll be more careful with my words."

"Yes, you will." He put his napkin on his plate and stood up. He'd already paid the bill, so he held out his arm for Berniece to take it. Seeing no other option, she slipped her hand into the curve of his arm, fully aware that people were watching them. She tried not to care, but she did. She didn't even want to be *seen* with this man, let alone be married to him.

They left the café and walked the short distance toward her home. "I'll work on coming up with just the right punishment for your words. I'll let you know what I've decided on when we see each other Saturday night. Then you can anticipate what will happen to you for the two months leading up to our wedding." He seemed extremely proud of his suggestion.

She felt like vomiting. Finally, she'd managed to say to him what she thought should be said, and this was his reaction. She could not marry this man. Ever. "All right."

"I look forward to the day when you are my wife and I can turn you over my knee and paddle you as you deserve. Your parents have been much too lax with you, Berniece." He stopped in front of her house. "Invite me inside."

She nodded. "Would you like to come inside, Mr. Chase?" She didn't dare disobey him at this point.

"And that adds a little more to whatever punishment I decide upon. I've told you repeatedly to call me Albert." He opened the door and went into the parlor, where both of her parents were sitting. Her father smiled, obviously pleased they were together, while her mother didn't look up from her needlepoint.

Berniece sat on one end of the sofa, hoping that Albert would sit on the far end. She'd have chosen a chair, but her parents occupied the only two chairs in the room.

"Did you have a nice time?" her father asked.

Berniece wanted to scream that it had been awful, but she let Albert answer for her instead, which he did as he sat in the middle of the couch, making sure his body was against hers. "You haven't done a very good job of teaching your daughter to be obedient, George. It's going to be my pleasure to teach her how to speak to her husband." The slow smile that crossed his face had Berniece stuffing her fist against her mouth to cover the gag that wanted to erupt.

George smiled. "I'm sure you'll take *great* pleasure in that." He nodded toward Berniece's mother. "I remember teaching Mary the same sorts of lessons when we were first married." He let out a booming laugh. "Sometimes I still spank her, just so she remembers. She doesn't even have to do anything wrong." He smiled at his wife affectionately. "Don't I, Mary?"

Mary made a slight nod of her head, still not looking up from her needlepoint. Berniece made a mental note to herself that her mother opposed the marriage. She'd have to find a time to speak with her alone. Perhaps she could convince her mother that this marriage wasn't in her best interests. She couldn't imagine her mother actually helping her get away, because she never defied her father, but maybe she could find some sympathy there at least.

Albert laughed as well. "I hope you know that I'll do what it takes to turn Berniece into a good wife." He reached over and covered Berniece's hand with his. "And now we'd like a moment alone for some sparking if you don't mind."

Berniece minded. She wanted to scream that she needed her parents to stay, but she knew that would *not* go over well at all.

George nodded. "Come along, Mary."

Berniece's mother looked up for the first time since they'd entered the room. Her eyes were blank. "Yes, dear." She followed her husband from the room, not looking even once at her daughter.

Albert turned to Berniece. "That's how you'll behave toward me soon. I will not allow your disobedience and rude ways to continue." He gripped her shoulders tightly as he slammed his mouth down onto hers. It was a punishing kiss, and there was no doubt in her mind that it was deliberate for the way she'd spoken to him.

When he finished, he grinned and wiped a trace of blood away from her mouth with his finger. "I'll go now. I want you to dream about what punishments you have in store for you, my dear." With those words, he stood up and headed for the door. "Just two months until our wedding. I'm counting down the days."

As soon as he'd left, Berniece buried her face in her hands and cried. How did her parents expect her to marry that monster?

BERNIECE MANAGED TO corner her mother the following morning. She spoke to her softly as they washed the dishes together. "I'm not sure I can marry Mr. Chase. He's not a kind man."

"Neither is your father. It's a woman's lot in life to marry whatever man her father chooses for her. I tried to talk your father into a man closer to your age who wasn't as . . . cruel, but he refused. You have no choice but to marry him." Her mother handed her a plate to dry. She'd obviously given up on helping her only child.

"But, Mama, surely you can see that marrying him would ruin my life. I have bruises on my shoulders from where he squeezed them last night."

Her mother closed her eyes for a moment. "I'm very sorry to hear that, Berniece, but there's nothing I can do."

Berniece nodded. She knew her mother would help her if it all possible, so it must not be possible. "Do you mind if I go to the mercantile today? I would like to see if I can find a new novel or perhaps a book of poetry." Her reading took her away from her life and transported her to a place that was free of abusive men. She needed another book or twelve to make it through the next week.

Her mother nodded. "Of course, you may." After a moment, her mother added, "I wish I could help you, Berniece. I can't, though. Surely you can see that."

"I do see that, Mama. Thank you for letting me go to the store." At least she would have a few minutes alone, during which she could walk around town, pretending she was engaged to a man she could actually love. Her imagination was all she had left.

An hour later, the dishes were done and her household chores for the day had been accomplished, so she put on a stylish hat and headed to the mercantile. The store was a fifteen-minute walk, and she enjoyed every moment of it, passing by people on the streets who didn't know her or only knew her a little. She nodded at everyone as they walked along, in her own little world.

At the mercantile, she lingered in the back, reading all the notices on the bulletin board. Each one of them gave her something to daydream about. One family needed a nanny for their daughter, and she imagined moving in with them and taking care of the little girl while she hid her whereabouts from her family and Albert. It wouldn't work, of course, but the idea was perfectly lovely.

At the bottom of the bulletin board was a notice she had seen many times in the past but never actually considered. "Mail Order Bride agency needs women who are looking for the adventure of their lives. Men out West need women to marry. Reply in person at 300 Rock Creek Road. See Mrs. Elizabeth Tandy."

She stared at the ad for a full five minutes before she chose a book of poetry, paid, and left the mercantile. Instead of heading for home, she walked toward Rock Creek Road, wondering if she'd have the courage to actually go to the door and speak with Mrs. Tandy. She knew she had to try. She had no other choice. A life with Robert Chase was the last thing she wanted or needed in her life.

When she got to the door, she took a deep breath and knocked, waiting for someone to answer. A tall blond man stood looking at her for a moment. She fought to get the words past her throat. Usually she wasn't a meek person, but she was so terribly afraid of everything that could go wrong, she couldn't find words. "I'm here to see Mrs. Tandy."

"Yes, of course." He opened the door for her. "I'm Bernard Tandy." Leading her down a long hallway to the last room on the left, he knocked softly on the open door. "Elizabeth?"

A beautiful woman, who was obviously very pregnant, stood up and walked toward them. "Hello. I'm Elizabeth Tandy. Please come in and have a seat." Then she turned her attention to the man there. "Would you bring us some tea and cookies? I have a feeling we have a lot to talk about."

Bernard smiled and nodded. "I'll see to it."

Elizabeth returned to the seat behind the desk and slowly lowered herself into her chair. She waited for a moment for Berniece to say something, but finally she spoke after a long silence. "You're here about the ad."

Berniece nodded. "I am." She was glad there was no one listening to them as she leaned forward earnestly. "I'm in desperate need of your help. My father is forcing me to marry a man who is more than thirty years older than I am. I suggested he marry someone closer to his age, and he's talked about nothing but punishing me since. I have bruises on my shoulders, and he made my lip bleed last night when he kissed me." She shook her head. "He actually seemed pleased to see the blood. I cannot spend my life with a man like that."

Elizabeth frowned, shaking her head. "No, you can't. How will your parents feel about you marrying someone else, though?"

"They won't allow it. That's why I need to find a way to get out. I'll have to leave in the dead of night. Well, my mother probably wouldn't say anything if I left during the day, but my father isn't much different than Albert."

Elizabeth's eyes widened. "Albert Chase?"

"Yes, I take it you know him?"

"Yes, I do. Unfortunately, I've had business dealings with him. You're right. You have to leave, and you have to do it quickly." Elizabeth pursed her lips as if thinking about it. "You won't be able to take much. Do you have a carpet bag? If not, I can give you one. You'll want to fill it with only clothing and leave just as soon as we can manage. I'll wait up for you tonight. Pack your things and come here as soon as your parents are asleep."

Berniece sagged against the back of the sofa. "I'll have to get out of town quickly. They'll be looking for me." She was so thankful she'd found someone who wanted to help her that she couldn't express it. She wanted to jump up and hug Elizabeth, thanking her for even considering her problem.

"Yes, they will." Elizabeth reached for a stack of papers on her desk. "I think I know just the situation for you. My younger sister, Charlie, is married to a man in Montana. His brother needs a wife, and if it doesn't work out between the two of you, Charlie will help you. I know she will." She pulled two letters from a stack and handed them to Berniece. "One is from Charlie, and one is from Kane, the man in question. Read them and tell me if Kane sounds like a man you could be happy with. Either way, I'll send you to Charlie, and she'll help you."

Berniece read the letter from Charlie first, and she smiled. "He sounds like he's a good man." Then she flipped to the letter from Kane, and she frowned.

Dear Potential Bride,

I'm looking for a mother for my daughter, who is not quite six months old. My wife died in childbirth. I'm not looking for a wife. I've had one, and she's dead. I want someone who will be a mother and nothing more. You will be expected to cook, clean, and care for my child, but there is nothing more that will be expected of you. I will provide you a room of your own. I don't care what you look like or how old you are as long as you're willing to be a mother to my little girl.

I am a rancher in Montana, and the winters are brutal. I don't want you to come here looking for a fairy-tale ending to your journey, because it won't happen. I'm offering you a life of hard work and little else. If this sounds like what you want in life, then please, come to me.

Sincerely,

Kane Burton

Reading the letter once more, Berniece shook her head. "A woman would have to be truly desperate to respond to this letter." She gave a half laugh. "Good for him; I'm that desperate. Should I write him back?"

"Yes, write him. I'll send your letter with mine to my sister." Elizabeth smiled. "If you're not able to bring yourself to marry him, I'll make sure Charlie takes care of you."

"I won't back out of a marriage with him. He's saving me from Mr. Chase." Berniece accepted the writing materials the older woman offered and quickly wrote a letter. "When will I leave?"

"I'll make sure that letter goes out in today's post, and you can leave tomorrow or the day after."

"My parents have a party tomorrow night. It will be easier for me to sneak out during the party than it will while they're sleeping."

Elizabeth smiled. "That's perfect. I will have one of the bedrooms readied for you, and we'll see to your train ticket today."

"Thank you so much." Berniece didn't even have the words to express how grateful she was to the other woman for getting her out of the situation she found herself in. She finished her letter and passed it to Elizabeth. "I'll see you tomorrow evening, then."

"Oh, if you can, you need to stay for tea and cookies. I'm sure Bernard will be back with them in a moment."

Berniece tilted her head to one side. "Is Bernard your husband or your butler?"

"He's both. He started out as my butler and bodyguard, and we married, but he kept doing the butler and bodyguard work. He said he wouldn't know what to do being a man of leisure."

The cookies arrived then, and Berniece took one as well as the tea Elizabeth poured into a delicate china cup for her. "Thank you."

"You're very welcome. I took over this business so I could help people like you, and I usually go to the train station with my brides, but I'd rather not walk that far in my condition," Elizabeth said, putting her hand over her stomach. "So, I'll tell you what I tell women right before they get on their trains for their journeys. If anything goes wrong with this marriage . . . and you discover your new husband doesn't treat you properly, you only have to write to me. I will send you a train ticket to come right back. Though, in your case, it might be best if you just talk to my sister. She'll help you."

Berniece smiled. "Thank you. That's the kind of reassurance I need. There is no doubt in my mind how I would be treated if I stayed here."

"There's none in mine either. You need to be careful when you marry. Men will take advantage." Elizabeth sighed as she finished her cookie, and Berniece got to her feet. "I believe that now our business is finished, I will have Bernard mail these letters for me, and I will take to my bed. Naps have become my new favorite thing with this child weighing so heavily on me."

"I hope you have many children with little pain," Berniece said. "I will see you tomorrow evening."

"Yes, you will. Be safe, my friend." Elizabeth walked Berniece to the door, frowning after her. As soon as she was out of sight, she turned to Bernard, whom she knew would be behind her. "Make sure Albert Chase doesn't follow her when she comes here tomorrow night. I'm afraid this one is going to need an armed escort to the train station. That man is *not* worthy of her."

Bernard shook his head. "No, he's not." He wrapped his arms around his wife from behind, his hands resting on her belly. "I will mail your letters while you rest. My babe is making you tired."

Elizabeth leaned back against him. "I do love you, Bernard Tandy."

Chapter Two

THE FOLLOWING EVENING while her parents were attending a party, Berniece took the carpet bag she'd already packed and headed out the back door. She was afraid of being seen, and even though it was past dark, she had to be extremely careful. She wouldn't be surprised if Albert Chase had men watching the house while her parents were away.

She'd left her engagement ring on her dresser—along with a note to her parents about leaving rather than marrying Mr. Chase—but she knew it wouldn't be found until the following morning. Her parents wouldn't check on her when they arrived home, and her mother wouldn't look in on her until late in the morning, because she believed she should be able to sleep as late as she wanted until she married and was forced to follow someone else's schedule.

She arrived at the Tandy house and knocked on the door, looking over her shoulder. She felt like someone had followed her. She knew it was probably just her nervousness, but she was genuinely afraid.

Bernard opened the door to her. "Miss Johnson, come in. I've had a room readied for you on the second floor." He led her up the stairs to a small bedroom. "Would you care to have a bath? I can have one drawn for you."

Berniece smiled. "No, thank you. I just want to sleep."

"That's understandable. Your train leaves at eight tomorrow morning, so I will have you woken at six if that works for you."

She smiled. That meant she would be on the train and most likely out of Massachusetts before her parents realized she was missing. Thank God. "That sounds wonderful. Thank you, Mr. Tandy."

"Please, call me Bernard. Elizabeth will be awake to see you off, and I believe we should head to the station around half-past seven. I will be driving you, so there is less chance you will be seen. My wife has given me a hat for you to wear so that it will be hard to recognize you."

"Thank you. It seems you are well-versed in the subterfuge of helping young ladies escape less-than-desirable circumstances." Once the words were spoken, she realized how he must have come by his experience, and she was saddened.

He nodded. "Unfortunately, I've had to become good at sneaking around." He looked around her room. "Is there anything else I can get for you this evening? There's a bath with a water closet through that door."

"I'll be fine. Thank you." Berniece closed the door and sat on the edge of her bed. The uncertainty of her future was almost welcome at that moment. At least it meant she couldn't possibly be forced to marry Albert Chase.

As she readied herself for bed, she thought about the little girl she was traveling to. A child who needed a mommy. She could be that mommy.

THE TRAIN RIDE WAS long and tiresome, and Berniece had never felt quite as alone as she did sitting in her seat and watching the world go by out the window of the train. It was humbling to realize she'd had to flee everything she'd ever known to avoid being married to a terrible man.

When the train was finally pulling into the station in Missoula, Montana, Berniece was exhausted. She hadn't slept in days, thanks to the bumpy ride the train offered and the couple who argued non-stop right behind her. She was ready to get off the train, but she wasn't ready to meet her future husband.

Getting off the train, she stepped onto the platform, aware that everything she owned was in a bag that she could lift with one hand.

She should have more, but she didn't, and it was slightly embarrassing for her to be going to a husband that way. She thought longingly for a moment about the wedding dress and trousseau her mother had commissioned back in Beckham, but that was part of another life. A life she had no desire for and no need for.

She looked around her for a moment, wondering where Kane was, but the only person she saw was a young woman holding an infant. Approaching her, she said, "I'm looking for Kane Burton. Do you know where I might find him?"

The woman's face lit up. "I'm Charlie Burton. Are you Berniece?"

"Yes, I am. Oh, thank goodness someone was here to meet me. I was afraid I'd beaten the letters that Elizabeth and I sent here." Berniece felt a wave of relief pass through her. "No Kane?"

Charlie shook her head. "He's working today. I think he'll come by tonight and meet you, and the two of you will marry tomorrow. The pastor is aware of your arrival."

Berniece was relieved not to have to meet Kane immediately, and she looked at the infant in the other woman's arms. "And this must be Kane's baby? I'm afraid I don't know her name."

"It's Ruth. Ruth, this is your new mommy."

The baby looked at Berniece, but she was quiet as she stared at her with her big blue eyes.

"It's nice to meet you Ruth." She held her hands out for the baby, but the little girl turned and buried her face in Charlie's shoulder. "She'll get used to me." Berniece had dreamed of the instant where she would see the baby and the child would immediately know her for her mother. Of course, that was just her imaginings, but she'd hoped the child would at least want to come to her.

"It's time for her nap," Charlie said by way of explanation. "It looks like you could use a nap as well. Is that all you have?" She nodded to the bag in Berniece's hand.

"Yes, I didn't have the ability to bring more."

Charlie smiled. "I understand completely. Come with me, and I'll show you where you can sleep."

"Are you sure? I can help around the house or something . . ."

"You're not here to be my maid." Charlie put the baby into a buggy, and the two of them walked through the streets of Missoula. "It's already getting cold as autumn rolls in. I hope you brought a coat."

"I did." It was one of the few things Berniece had shoved into the carpet bag. She knew she could make new dresses, but a new coat would be a great deal more expensive. "Tell me about Kane."

Charlie sighed. "Well, you know he lost his wife in childbirth. Ruth has stayed with us ever since. We found her a wet nurse who lived with my husband and me. She actually left on a train not thirty minutes ago. She's been the closest thing little Ruth has had to a mother."

"What was Kane's wife like? I worry I won't be able to measure up."

"She was very pretty," Charlie said after what seemed like a long pause. "Ruth takes after her."

Berniece nodded, waiting for more, but when the other woman said nothing else, she moved on. "And Kane's ranch?"

"Oh, it's a huge ranch. He raises cattle, but he has chickens and a milk cow as well. You'll be able to get many things you need to cook right there on the ranch. And we do have a well-supplied mercantile for things like flour, sugar, and other cooking staples." Charlie stopped at a large, pretty house. "Here we are. I hope you and I will be good friends." She opened the door and let the other woman precede her into the house.

"Your home is lovely," Berniece said, feeling a little out of place. She hoped Kane didn't have the kind of wealth his brother had.

"Thank you. I like it a great deal. Abel and I only married about seven months ago. MaryAnn and I made up the room she's been sleeping in, and it will be yours tonight and any other night you feel the need to stay in town. Sometimes it's easier to stay here during a storm." She picked the baby up out of the buggy and carried her upstairs, leaving Berniece to follow her. "If you're hungry, I can make something up for lunch really quick, but you look a great deal more tired than hungry."

"I am. I had a sandwich on the train a few hours ago. All I want to do right now is sleep for a few hours. The train ride was awful." Berniece didn't want to complain, but she was so tired, she barely knew what was coming out of her mouth.

"I've made a train ride that long, and I completely understand. I was with a friend and two children, which helped me not feel so lonely, but I can't imagine doing it alone." Charlie shook her head, opening a door to a room with a bed and a crib. "I hope you won't mind that the baby sleeps in here. It was easier for her to be in the same room with MaryAnn."

"Of course not. I look forward to getting acquainted with her." Berniece felt a pull toward the baby, which pleased her. Even if she never had feelings for the baby's father, at least she would have the opportunity to be a mommy. "Did you say your husband's name is Abel?"

"Yes, I'm sure you're thinking what I thought when I met him. The two brothers are named Kane and Abel. When I heard, I was appalled. Their father was not a believer, and he thought it would be funny to name them after the brothers from the Bible. They're strange names for brothers, but I promise they love each other."

"I see. Yes, those are very strange names. What about Kane? Is he a believer?"

"Yes, he is. You don't have any worries there."

"I'm glad to hear it." Berniece sat down on the bed, rubbing her eyes. "How long will the baby nap?"

"Oh, not more than an hour or two," Charlie told her. "I'll keep an ear out for her, and when she wakes, I'll hurry in and get her. We have her on an infant food mixed with cow's milk. MaryAnn and I have spent a month teaching her to drink from a bottle, so she could get used to it."

"What happened to MaryAnn's child?" Berniece asked quietly.

Charlie shook her head sadly. "She lost her husband in an accident, and a short while later gave birth to a stillborn baby. She came to us the next day, and she has lived with us ever since. She began a correspondence with a childhood sweetheart who lives near her mother, and she's chosen to go back east to live with family. She needs to start a new life, and being a wet nurse was doing nothing toward that."

"I can see that." Berniece looked over at the baby, who was now lying in her crib sound asleep. "Sounds like that little girl has already had a lot of upheaval in her life. I plan to be a constant for her."

"I'm glad. She and Kane need someone strong to mend their lives. I do hope you'll be patient with him. He's had a very trying time."

"Of course, I will!" Berniece shook her head. "His letter made me feel a great deal of sadness for him."

Charlie smiled. "Elizabeth told me a little about what you had to run away from in Massachusetts. I think you'll find Montana very healing. I know I have." She got to her feet and went to the door. "I'll see you when you wake up or when the baby wakes up. Please don't worry about getting up to care for her, because I'll do it. You need to rest up for being a mother."

Berniece nodded, curling into a ball on her side, not bothering to remove any of her clothing. What she needed the most was sleep, and it came soon after she closed her eyes.

WHEN BERNIECE WOKE, it was already getting dark. She sat up straight in the bed she'd been given and got to her feet. The baby was out of her crib, and she was mortified that she'd slept through her crying. She went to the pitcher and bowl and splashed water on her face, fixing her hair in the attached mirror. Then she hurried downstairs, hoping Charlie wouldn't think poorly of her.

She found the other woman in the kitchen with two men, one of whom was holding the baby. "I'm so sorry for sleeping that long. I meant to wake up when the baby cried, but I must have slept through it."

Charlie turned from the stove, where she had a huge pot of stew cooking. "Don't worry about it. I know how exhausting that train is." She smiled over her shoulder at Berniece. "This is my husband Abel, and his brother, Kane, is the one holding the baby."

Berniece nodded first at Abel and then at Kane. "It's nice to meet you both. I'm sorry I wasn't awake when you got here."

Abel laughed. "You've got to be exhausted after traveling so far. Charlie didn't mind."

Kane merely nodded at her, seeming to study her. He held the baby against his chest, as if he wanted to protect her from the world.

"I was tired, but now I probably won't sleep tonight," Berniece said with a self-deprecating laugh. "I should have asked you to wake me after an hour or two."

Charlie shrugged. "I wouldn't have done it. I could see you needed your sleep." She turned from the stove. "And supper's ready. I hope you're hungry."

Both of the men walked toward the dining room, and Kane put the baby into a high chair. When Charlie came in, she put a piece of bread crust onto the tray for the baby. Berniece carried two bowls to the table, feeling as if she should have helped with the meal. Charlie came in right after her, carrying two more bowls of stew, and then hurried out for a cutting board with a loaf of bread and a small ball of butter.

Berniece sat with the others, feeling inept and out of place. She hated that she'd slept so long. As soon as they were all seated, Abel said a quick prayer, and then the four of them ate while the baby chomped at the heel of the bread.

"How was your trip?" Abel asked Berniece, and she quickly swallowed her bite of stew to answer him.

"It was long and tedious. I wish I'd had time to get a few books for the journey, but there was no way I could do that and get on a train when I did."

Kane looked at her, speaking for the first time. "I'm glad you came when you did. I wouldn't have wanted Charlie to feel burdened taking care of the baby on her own."

Charlie sighed. "I've told you a hundred times that Ruth will never be a burden for me. I couldn't love her more if she were my own."

Kane smiled at his sister-in-law. "Thank you for treating her as if she was your own. It's a great deal more than I should have expected from my brother's wife." He looked over at Berniece as if sizing her up. "And you'll take on the burden of caring for her now. Charlie shouldn't feel the need to step in at all."

Berniece nodded. "I plan to. I feel badly that I slept so long, but I didn't get any sleep on the train." She hoped he wasn't judging her for not helping with the baby and with supper, but she felt as if he was.

"Be that as it may, whether you sleep or not, the baby is now your responsibility."

Berniece felt as if she'd been put in her place. She hoped he wasn't the kind of man who would insist on punishing her as Albert Chase would have. "I won't let sleep keep me from my duties again."

"See that you don't." Kane resumed eating, but he kept watching Berniece, as if he was expecting her to get up and dance a jig or do something else equally interesting.

Charlie looked back and forth between the two of them, looking a little uncomfortable. "The pastor is willing to do the wedding at two tomorrow afternoon. I thought we could do a small meal here after, if you don't mind, Kane."

"I don't mind."

Berniece smiled. "I would love to help you prepare the meal."

Charlie smiled and nodded. "That sounds good. It'll be nice to have a sister around again."

Abel smiled. "I'm closing my shop at one tomorrow so that I can be there for your wedding. I'm excited to see you finally married off to a good woman."

Berniece thought Abel had emphasized the word good for a moment, but decided she must be imagining things. There was no way Abel could be saying Kane's first wife hadn't been a good woman, could there? "I'll do my best to live up to expectations." Berniece had been cooking and helping her mother around the house since she was a little girl. She had no doubt that she would do just fine once she'd slept enough.

After supper, Berniece helped clear the table, and she washed the dishes. She was surprised when Charlie didn't join her, but Kane came in.

"I just want you to know that you will need to pull your weight. I'm not marrying you to add another burden to my life. You'll cook, clean, and mind the baby, no matter whether you feel like doing it or not."

Berniece frowned at him. "I have no problem doing those things. I just got no sleep on the train. If Charlie had woken me, I'd have helped her with no problem." She felt like Kane was judging her as lazy without ever giving her a chance to prove she wasn't like he thought she was.

"Then make sure she knows to wake you when it's time to do the chores in the morning. I don't want to hear that you didn't help at all." With those words, he left the room.

Berniece felt as if she was an inch tall. How could a man she'd never met make her feel so badly about herself? He wasn't fifty, but she wasn't sure he was better than Albert in any other way.

When she joined Charlie and Abel in the parlor, it was to find that Kane had already left for the night. Berniece wasn't sure what his problem was, but he was making it clear she wasn't there to be his wife. She was only there to cook and clean and take care of his child. Nothing more. She'd gotten the same feeling from his letter, but somehow, she'd been sure it would all work out in the end. Now she was much more certain she would spend her life unloved.

Chapter Three

BERNIECE WOKE EARLY the following day, and she hurried downstairs to help with the preparations for the wedding. The baby was still sleeping, but she promised herself she'd be the one to get her out of bed and change her.

She found Charlie in the kitchen, humming as she mixed up the batter for a cake.

"How can I help?" she asked.

Charlie smiled. "Well, let's see. I'm planning on making roast beef for our after-wedding meal, so if you want to get that into the oven, that would be wonderful." She nodded her head toward the ice box.

"No problem." Berniece dug around until she found a large baking dish and put the pot roast into the oven. "Are we doing potatoes and carrots?" she asked.

"Well, of course. But let's not peel those until shortly before the wedding." Charlie poured the batter into a cake pan. "Now, let's talk about the baby. I'm assuming you're experienced enough with babies to at least know how to change a diaper?"

Berniece nodded. "I've changed many at the orphanage in Beckham. I volunteered there before my father arranged my marriage and I was expected to spend every waking moment planning for my wedding day."

"Good. I'm glad you've at least got some experience with babies. Let me show you how we mix her milk." Charlie led her to the sink and showed her the process. "I warm the milk in a pan, but just so it's my body temperature, and then we pour it into a bottle for her." Charlie demonstrated as she explained. "Now, we're ready for her when she wakes up, and if she's true to form, it'll be within the next ten minutes. That child has herself on a schedule, and she likes it that way."

Charlie put some oatmeal into bowls for them both. "Now we eat, while we wait for her to cry."

"Does she eat oatmeal?" Berniece asked.

"Yes, but she has to be fed. She can eat things like a crust of bread by herself, because she's really just gnawing on it, but actual food we want inside her needs to be spoon fed."

"That makes sense." Berniece heard the baby cry, and she got to her feet. "I want to start taking care of her with you here, so you can let me know if I need to do anything differently. Kane made it clear that she's my responsibility and mine alone."

"I'm sure he did," Charlie said, shaking her head. "Don't worry about him. He'll come around."

Berniece hurried out of the kitchen, feeling a tear pop into her eye. She'd escaped a terrible situation, and she knew she should be grateful for this opportunity, but she still felt very vulnerable. When she got to the room she'd slept in, she picked the baby up and patted her back. "I'm here, Ruth. Everything will be all right."

The baby watched her warily as she changed her diaper, probably wondering why this new person was taking care of her. Berniece diapered her and carried her downstairs, talking to her softly. "Are you hungry? Your auntie Charlie and I made you a bottle." When she got to the kitchen, she picked up the bottle and fed the little girl. Ruth sucked at the bottle as if she'd been doing it her entire life, and Berniece smiled down at her. "She takes the bottle well."

"She didn't at first," Charlie said, smiling at her niece. "She had to learn. She loved nursing, and taking that bottle made her very angry at first. The past month has been rough as we've taught her to take only the bottle. MaryAnn needed to be free to go home."

"I'm sure you miss her." Berniece stared down at the little girl in her arms,

"I do. I didn't expect to become as close to her as I did, and I'll be forever grateful she was here with me through Ruth's first months. When she decided to leave, I knew I had to write Elizabeth and get her to find someone to marry Kane. He was resistant—not wanting to marry so soon—but I think he knows it's the right thing for Ruth."

"He doesn't seem to want me around at all," Berniece said sadly.

"His relationship with Veronica was tumultuous, and I think you'll find that he warms up to you as the days go by. Just be the best mother and housewife you can be, and things will all work out."

Tumultuous? Berniece wasn't sure Charlie knew what she was talking about. From his letter, it seemed to her that Kane was still infatuated with his late wife.

"I hope so," Berniece said, sitting the baby up and burping her. "It's going to be strange to be married to a man who doesn't want me there. I was afraid I'd be married to a man who wanted me *too much*."

Charlie frowned. "Lizard Breath said you were supposed to marry a man who disgusts you. I hope you don't feel the same way about Kane."

Berniece had to chuckle at the nickname Charlie used for her sister. "He doesn't disgust me, but I feel like I disgust him. I wish I knew what to do to make him realize I'm not lazy. That's what he thinks after I slept all day yesterday."

"I told him how tired you were after that train ride! I don't know what that man's problem is, but he's going to get a piece of my mind."

Berniece shook her head adamantly. "No. We need to work it out between us."

"All right. But I would be happy to intervene if you think it'll help."

"I think it would just make things worse at this point. After a week or two, he'll get to know me better and see that I'm capable of keeping up with the housework and the baby, and things will be better. I just have to prove myself to him." Berniece shrugged, giving the baby a bite of her oatmeal. "Veronica must have been a wonderful housewife, and he's holding me up to her standards. It sounds like she was practically perfect." Charlie choked on her oatmeal, and Berniece gave her a worried look. "Are you all right?"

"I'm fine." Charlie took a big drink of her water, swallowing hard.

"So, do we have a pretty dress for the baby for the wedding?" Berniece didn't even have a pretty, new dress for herself, but she had something that would do.

Charlie nodded emphatically. "I made it myself. It's a beautiful white dress, and she looks darling in it."

After breakfast, Berniece put the baby in her high chair with a couple of spoons to make noise with, and she happily pounded away while the two women got ready for their wedding supper.

"Is it just going to be the four of us?" Berniece asked.

"Yes. Kane doesn't feel right making your wedding a big production, since it hasn't even been a year since Veronica died." Charlie didn't meet Berniece's eyes when she said that, and Berniece felt like there was something she was missing out on, but she had no idea what it could be.

Berniece mixed the dough for a loaf of bread while Charlie drank some water.

"Excuse me," Charlie said, running from the room.

When she returned, Berniece looked at her. "Are you all right?"

"Morning sickness. I'll be happy when that part of this pregnancy is over."

"Oh! You're expecting! I had no idea." Berniece was genuinely happy for the other woman.

"Yes, I am, and I'm thrilled. Ruth needs cousins, don't you think?"

"I do think so. I'm not sure her father will ever agree to brothers and sisters for her." It wasn't just that his first wife had died in childbirth, but he'd made it plain he didn't think much of Berniece.

"Oh, I think that will change pretty quickly. Kane loves children."

"He does?" Berniece was surprised. It was hard to imagine the man she was going to marry having any kind of positive emotion at all. He seemed very stoic and angry to her.

"He does. Ruth is the light of his life. You'll see. If he's not with her, he's talking about her. I don't think I've ever seen such a devoted father."

"Well, with as much as he obviously loved her mother, it makes sense. He probably sees Veronica in little Ruth."

"Maybe." Charlie didn't sound convinced. It didn't matter, though, because Berniece could see the writing on the wall, and she knew very well where she stood.

By the time the men arrived to walk with them to the church, all three girls were dressed in their Sunday best. Berniece loved the look on little Ruth's face when her daddy got there; the baby excitedly tried to dive out of her arms toward her favorite man. She hadn't quite realized there was already such a bond with the two of them living separately, but the girl obviously knew who her father was.

Berniece was dressed in navy blue, and her hair was in an intricate knot atop her head, thanks to Charlie's help. As they walked, the two women walked together, and the two men walked ahead of them with Ruth in her father's arms. When they reached the church, Berniece said a silent prayer for strength. She wasn't sure she was doing the right thing, but little Ruth had already captured Berniece's heart, and she *had* to go through with it.

At the front of the church, the pastor quickly went through the ceremony, and Berniece was surprised at how quickly it all went. When Kane was told to kiss his bride, he looked uncertain for a moment before he leaned down and pressed a kiss to Berniece's cheek. She wanted to yell at him for not caring enough to even kiss her properly, but she couldn't.

As soon as it was over, they thanked the pastor and made their way back to Abel and Charlie's house, where their feast awaited them.

They ate their meal and then had cake, and after Berniece helped Charlie to clean up, Kane went out to hitch up his wagon and bring it around. He and Abel carried the crib and the high chair out to the wagon and then all of the baby's things. Berniece had expected the baby to stay in town for a couple of more days as she and Kane got used to each other, but that wasn't a plan anyone else had.

She carried the baby out to the wagon, and he took the child, holding her while Berniece climbed onto the wagon seat. It was her first time to climb up with no help, and she was certain her skirts would become tangled, but she made it up, holding out her hands for the baby.

Berniece held Ruth close as Kane climbed up beside her and flicked the leads. Waving goodbye to Charlie, Berniece hoped she would see the other girl often. She'd already formed a bond with Charlie, and she hated the idea of not having her friend close.

Kane made the five-minute drive out into the country in silence, pulling up in front of a pretty two-story white house. After getting down, he took Ruth, and once Berniece was on the ground beside him, he handed the baby back over. He said nothing else as he worked to carry in the baby's things, leaving her to carry her carpet bag along with the baby.

When she stepped foot inside the house, she swallowed hard. It was positively filthy. She didn't even want to let the baby sit anywhere, but then she remembered that the high chair was clean. She put the baby into it and rolled up her sleeves. Cleaning up months' worth of dust and dirt was not how she'd planned to spend her wedding day, but there was truly no choice in the matter. It needed to be done, and so she would do it. She was the wife and new mother, which meant it was now her responsibility.

Kane came in after unhitching the wagon and took the baby from the high chair. She started to tell him not to put the baby down until she'd finished cleaning, but he sat with the baby on his lap in a rocking chair.

It took her hours, but she got the kitchen clean enough that she felt like she could make meals there that wouldn't make them all ill, and she finally sat down at the table, utterly and completely exhausted. She hadn't had enough sleep all week, and since she'd gotten up that morning, she'd been cooking or cleaning. Surely, he would understand her exhaustion now.

"I put the crib in the baby's room upstairs," Kane told her. "Charlie sent home the quilt she'd made for her, so everything in the crib is clean."

"Good. I'll tackle everything else tomorrow."

He studied her for a moment before nodding. "I'll show you the room that will be yours." He led her up the stairs, still carrying the baby. "This room is hers." He pushed open a door, and the crib was in the room along with a small dresser. There was nothing else in there. She wanted to ask if the baby's mother had made her anything for her room, but she couldn't, because the subject seemed to be taboo.

He led her down to another door. "And this will be your room."

The room he showed her was covered in dust like the downstairs had been, and she tried not to let her feelings show. The room would need to be cleaned thoroughly before she would feel comfortable sleeping there, but there was nowhere else. She definitely had her work cut out for her. "This room will do nicely. Thank you."

Kane watched his pretty new wife, wondering how she was going to react to the filthy room he'd designated as hers, but she didn't complain, simply straightening her spine as if she was gearing up for more work. He had misjudged her the day before, and that was obvious now. She was a worker, plain and simple. He thought about apologizing for the way he'd spoken to her, but he found he preferred to leave things as they were. He didn't want them to be on good terms. She was there to take care of his daughter and feed him. Nothing else really mattered. "Good. I try to be on the range by half-past five, so breakfast at five would be nice. I will milk the cow and gather eggs at four thirty, so they'll be ready for you to make breakfast."

"Sounds good," Berniece said, already wanting to melt into a puddle on the floor as she thought about the long day she would have the next day, getting everything cleaned to her satisfaction and making sure meals were made. "I need to give the baby her bottle. Do you need to eat again?" She hoped his answer was no, because she wasn't sure she was up for cooking anything after all she'd done.

"Just some scrambled eggs would be nice. I don't have a lot of food in the house."

Berniece nodded. "I'll fix the baby's bottle and your eggs. Bring her down when you're ready to eat, please."

"I think she needs her diaper changed," he said, looking at her.

"Yes, of course." Berniece took the baby and changed her in her crib, not wanting to lay her on any other surface in the house. After changing Ruth, she handed the girl back to her father and headed down the stairs to make eggs and a bottle. Thankfully, Charlie had sent the infant food the girl needed.

After fixing meals for Kane and Ruth, she took the baby from her new husband and fed her, talking to her in an animated voice as she held her. "I'm so glad you like that food, because your new mommy doesn't have the ability to feed you any other way. No, I don't!"

Kane watched Berniece with the baby, and he knew she would be a good mother, even though she may not be a good wife. The two of them seemed natural together, and he was pleased to see it. As he plowed through his eggs, his mind was on the two girls in his life. "I'll be home at noon and six for meals. I expect them to be hot and ready when I ride up."

She nodded. "I'll take care of it."

"There are several ranch hands, but you won't be expected to feed them at all. Your entire job will be taking care of me and Ruth, feeding us, and making sure the house is clean."

"Yes, of course." Berniece wanted to throw something at him, but the only thing she had available was a baby bottle, and she didn't want to have to clean up the glass from the floor.

He tipped his head to one side as he watched her. "Whatever you're running away from back east must be pretty horrific if you were willing to marry a man who didn't want a wife."

She nodded. "It was. I was expected to marry a man thirty years older than me who was planning ways to punish me for pointing out that he might want a wife closer to his age. He left bruises on my shoulders before we were married. Imagine what he would have done after."

Kane frowned. "I'm not perfect, and I won't claim to be. But I promise I will not hurt you."

"That's all I'm looking for at the moment." With that, she pulled the bottle out of the baby's mouth and burped her. She was glad they understood one another.

Chapter Four

BERNIECE WOKE BEFORE the sun was up the following morning, peeking her head in at the baby before she stumbled down the stairs. She started a fire in the stove and immediately started a small pot of oatmeal for the baby. While that was cooking, she sliced bacon off of the big slab of meat she found in the ice box and started it frying. She located a coffee grinder and started a pot of coffee.

She put eggs on to fry as soon as she heard Kane moving around, and then sat down for a moment. The kitchen was the only clean room in the house for now, and that would need to change by the end of the day. She hadn't enjoyed sleeping in the dusty room that had been designated as hers, so she would need to wash all bed linens and get the rooms cleaned that day. Starting out her day in a state of exhaustion wasn't going to help her get the things she needed to do finished.

She had breakfast on the table by the time Kane came in from collecting the eggs and milking the cows. He immediately sat down to eat, saying nothing to her as he inhaled his breakfast.

She sat with him in silence for a moment. "I'm going to need to do a little shopping before I can do any real cooking," she said softly.

He nodded. "I figured that. If you want to walk into town with the baby, that would be fine, or wait for me. I could take an hour to do shopping with you on Monday."

"I don't know if the food we have on hand will be enough to make it until Monday. We really need several things."

He shrugged. "Make do or go on your own. If you decide to go, put the food on my account at the mercantile. Just explain you're my new wife." With that, he stood, plopped his hat on his head, and left for the day.

Berniece stared at the closed door, wondering what on earth was wrong with the man. He expected her to cook three meals a day, but he expected her to do it with no food. No one could manage that way—not even his *perfect* Veronica.

She had finished the breakfast dishes and given the baby her bottle and was feeding her oatmeal when there came a knock at the door. She was already close to tears, so if it wasn't a neighbor there to bring her a cake to welcome her, she didn't know if she was going to be able to manage not to cry.

She hurried to the door and threw it open, finding Charlie on the other side, and much to her chagrin, she did burst into tears immediately.

Charlie stepped inside, hugging Berniece. "I'm sure this house is a mess. I thought about coming to clean it before you came, but we were getting ready for MaryAnn to leave, and I just didn't have time."

Berniece nodded, wiping her face with her apron. "What brings you by?"

"Well, I brought you a loaf of bread, and I figured you would need help around the house today. Getting that much cleaning done while taking care of the baby is going to be difficult." Charlie walked over and picked up the spoon and oatmeal. "I'll feed the baby, and you do whatever you need to do next."

"Thank you. I need to wash bed linens and clean upstairs next, I think. And we need food. I don't know how Kane expects me to cook with no food in the house!"

"You get the laundry on the line, and I'll drive you into town for food. I brought the wagon, thinking you might need to make a trip to the mercantile."

Berniece smiled through her tears. "You're the best sister-in-law anyone could ever ask for. I'll get to work right now."

Two hours later, the laundry was on the line, and Charlie drove them into town. As soon as they reached the mercantile, she took the sleeping baby from Berniece's arms and waited while she hurried in to shop.

Berniece walked straight to the counter to speak with the proprietor, who was dusting the shelf, but he looked up when she stopped in front of him.

"I'm Berniece Burton. I just married Kane. He said you would let me put things on his account."

"Nice to meet you, Mrs. Burton. I'm Terrence Walker. Feel free to shop. I have no problem charging your husband's account." He returned to his dusting, and she wandered around the store, finding what she needed.

She had to start from scratch, because she couldn't find even a cup of flour in the house. He must have gotten rid of everything after Veronica died. It took her more than thirty minutes to choose everything she needed and have it charged to Kane's account. When she was done, Mr. Walker had his son carry everything out to the wagon.

After climbing back into the wagon—which was getting much easier on her own with practice—Berniece took the baby back from Charlie. "All right. Let's get home so I can have a hot meal on the table at noon as Kane requires."

Charlie shook her head. "Sounds like he's requiring a lot from you."

"Oh, he is, but I'll manage." Berniece looked down into the sweet face of the baby sleeping in her arms, and she knew she'd do anything to continue to be allowed to be this baby's mommy.

When they reached the house, Berniece sent Charlie in with the baby while she unloaded everything from the wagon. The bag of flour was heavy, and she had a hard time carrying it in, thrown over one shoulder. She dumped the flour inside the door and went back for more. It took her six trips to get everything into the house, and she sat down for a moment when she was done.

"I still need to cook lunch, but I need to catch my breath first." She glanced at the clock on the wall and saw that she had thirty minutes before Kane would be there for lunch.

"Let me get lunch taken care of. I'll make some bacon sandwiches, and he'll be just fine with that on your first day." Charlie took the baby upstairs and came back down to cook lunch while Berniece started working on the parlor.

"Thank you for coming to help me today," Berniece said softly. "I don't know what I would have done without you. I couldn't have slept in that bed one more night without washing the linens."

Charlie nodded. "I remember helping Veronica clean this house when she was very pregnant."

"I'm sure cleaning is hard when you're expecting, yet there you are helping me." Berniece shook her head. "I shouldn't let you help, but there is so much to do. Once I'm caught up, I won't need as much help as I do now."

"I know that. You can help me when the baby is born," Charlie said with a smile.

"I sure will." Berniece finished sweeping out the parlor, and then she dusted every surface. When she had finished those tasks, she started on the windows, which were filthy like everything else in the house.

She had just finished one of the windows and collapsed into a chair when Kane walked in the door.

Charlie put food on the table for the three of them, and Kane glared at Berniece. "I thought I made it clear that you were to be the one doing the work around here and not being a burden on Charlie."

Berniece bit her lip against what she wanted to say. There was no way she should open her mouth, because she had no idea what might come out of it at that moment.

Charlie set her sandwich down and looked at her brother-in-law. "I came here to offer my help, because I had an idea of what the state of this house would be. I'm glad I did, because I was able to help her with the baby and drive her into town for supplies. Shame on you, Kane Burton, expecting your new wife to do things that no woman possibly could. She needed help, and she got it. She's already agreed to help me when my baby is born, so you don't have to worry about her paying me back for it."

Kane frowned at Charlie before looking at Berniece. "This isn't going to be a habit, though. Is that understood?"

"I didn't ask for help. She came and offered it." Berniece kept her voice even, though she wanted to yell at him. Why did he keep assuming she was lazy? Had he not looked at all that had been done around the house since she'd gotten there? "Charlie made lunch, drove me to town, and held the baby. I've done everything else that's been done."

He looked around the house, noting that the dust that he'd started to think was permanent was completely gone. The windows had been washed, and the floors had been scrubbed. He'd noticed bed linens hanging on the line as well as diapers. "We'll talk about this later." And they would. She deserved an apology. He was painting her with the same brush Veronica had needed to be painted with, and it wasn't fair to her.

After lunch, he rode back out to work, but his mind was still on how unfairly he'd treated his wife. He needed to be kinder to her.

Berniece's afternoon was filled with more cleaning and cooking supper. She baked some fresh bread and even made a cake for dessert. Charlie helped with the baby, but she was mostly there to keep Berniece company as she worked.

"When you're all caught up on the house, we can spend a couple of afternoons together every week. We can talk or sew together while the baby sleeps."

Berniece smiled, nodding. "I would like that a lot. For now, I have a lot of mending to do and so much laundry. I only did diapers and linens today. I'll have a lot more to do on Monday." She was tired, but she felt good about everything she'd accomplished. Her fall cleaning was going to be completely finished within a week, and then she would feel as if she had the right to do what she wanted on the occasional afternoon.

"I brought you something as a housewarming gift," Charlie said before she left. "Let me get it."

Berniece waited as Charlie went out to her wagon and brought in something wrapped in a dish cloth. "My friend Merry made it, and I think you'll enjoy having it in your home."

Carefully unwrapping the package, Berniece cried out with pleasure. "Oh, it's beautiful. Did she carve it herself?" She turned the wooden sculpture over in her hands, noting that it was a grizzly bear, carefully carved from wood.

"Yes, she did. She's amazing." Charlie smiled. "I came to Montana with her when she needed help, and she and I formed a fast friendship. I think my sister is as much of a friend matcher as she is a matchmaker. Because here you are, and we're friends now, too."

Berniece smiled and nodded. "We are friends. Thank you for welcoming me with open arms the way you did. I'll never forget the kindness you've shown me."

"I won't let you," Charlie responded. "We're sisters-in-law, and I live just a five-minute drive from here." With a quick hug, Charlie was on her way, promising to see Berniece at church in a couple of days. Berniece was pleased she'd know at least one other woman who she could talk to. It would be nice to meet her new congregation with a friend at her side.

Berniece heard the baby then, and she climbed the stairs, lifting Ruth from her crib. "Are you hungry?" she asked, changing the baby's diaper. "Milk?"

The baby just looked at her as if she'd lost her mind with her questions, but Berniece noticed that she was settling more comfortably in her arms every time she held her. They would make a great team, her and Ruth, and she would teach her everything a woman needed to know about how to take care of her home.

When Kane walked in the door at the end of the day, he smelled fresh-baked bread and something more. He walked to the stove and looked into a pot of chicken and dumplings, and his stomach stood up and reminded him of how hungry he was.

"Sit down, and I'll serve it," Berniece said.

"I didn't notice you there."

"I was in the parlor with Ruth." She put the baby into her high chair and served them both a bowl of chicken and dumplings before carefully fishing out a dumpling for the baby. When she sat down, she waited for Kane to pray over their food, and then she took a small piece of dumpling from the baby's bowl, blew on it, and fed it to the little girl, whose mouth was open and ready.

She took turns feeding herself and feeding Ruth. She didn't notice as Kane finished his bowl, but she did see when he got up to serve himself another helping. "I'd have done that for you," she said, not wanting him to accuse her of being lazy again. She was anything but.

"You're taking care of the baby. I can refill my own bowl." He sat down, and now that the worst of his hunger was sated, he started the conversation he'd known he needed to have with her since lunchtime. "I want to apologize for being so hard on you. I didn't know that Charlie had come unexpectedly or that you were planning on helping her when the baby came. I just thought you were adding to her duties, and I saw red."

"I wouldn't. I didn't come out here to be a burden on anyone. That first day when I got off the train, I was so tired, I was stumbling a little when I walked, so when Charlie suggested I take a nap, I jumped at the chance. But I really thought I'd wake when the baby did. I guess I was even more tired than I realized." She shook her head. "But honestly, that's the only time I haven't pulled my own weight since I arrived. I've taken care of Ruth and done all the cleaning you've seen done. Charlie spent most of the day, but she held the baby and entertained her and kept me company while I worked."

"Will you forgive me for jumping to conclusions?" He thought briefly about telling her how Veronica had been, but he thought better of it. No, it was better if she thought he'd half-worshipped his first wife than she knew the truth of the matter. What if she took that as an invitation to be a wastrel as Veronica had?

Berniece nodded. "Thank you for apologizing. It's good to hear that you can see what I've been doing around here."

He picked up his fork and started on his second bowl of dumplings, watching how sweet she was with the baby. "Supper is delicious. Where did you learn to cook so well?"

She smiled at that. "My mother taught me that the most important skill a woman could have was cooking, and I learned at her side. She also taught me how to sew and clean. We had enough money for a servant when I was growing up, but my father felt like a wife who didn't bother to cook and clean was a waste of space, so Mother always did the chores herself."

"Well, I need to write a letter to your mother and thank her, then. This truly is an amazing meal."

Berniece frowned. "You know my parents don't know where I am, don't you?"

He shook his head. "I know you were running from an engagement you didn't want, but I thought you'd have at least told them where you went."

"I couldn't. My father would have dragged me back, kicking and screaming. I promise, this is the only way I could have come."

"So, did you sneak out in the middle of the night?" he asked, surprised.

"No, but what I did isn't much better. I packed my things, and as soon as my parents went to a party, I left. I did leave them a note along with my engagement ring on the dresser in my room, but they have no idea where I was going or what I was doing. I had no desire to ever even look at that ring again."

"Was the match they chose for you that bad?"

"Much worse than I can even express. I know they're looking for me, and I pray they never find me." She looked at Ruth as she carefully fed her another bite. "I want so much more for our baby than my parents ever wanted for me."

He frowned at her use of "our." Already she was seeing little Ruth as her own. He wasn't sure if that was a good thing or a bad thing, but it did make him feel just a tad bit guiltier. Berniece was a better mother than Veronica ever would have been. There was no doubt in his mind. And how was he supposed to not feel guilty for knowing that? Veronica hadn't wanted the "thing growing inside her." And here Berniece was willing to take on the burden of another woman's child without second thought.

Chapter Five

BERNIECE WOKE UP THE following morning, aching in every part of her body. She rolled out of bed and dressed in the dark, knowing she needed to keep going even though she wanted nothing more than to give up. If only Kane acted like he appreciated all the hard work she did, things would be easier. At least he'd apologized for acting like she was lazy, but she was fed up with the situation—after only a couple of days.

She checked on the baby before going downstairs to start breakfast. Now that she had fresh bread, she'd do bacon, eggs, and toast. At least she had a little bit of butter Charlie had brought with the bread the day before.

She started the fire in the stove and ground the coffee beans, her arm aching with every turn of the crank. She was surprised at just how much it hurt until she thought about all she'd done the day before. The house was almost completely put to rights because she'd worked from the moment she'd woken up until she'd gone to sleep. Maybe Kane had apologized for assuming she was lazy, but he certainly hadn't thanked her for cleaning up almost an entire year's worth of dust and dirt. She hoped it was only a year. Veronica may have been a slob, but from the way Kane talked, that would be hard for her to believe.

Pushing through the pain, she took her anger out on the coffee beans. She knew the man wouldn't hit her, so she wasn't afraid of him, and she also wasn't afraid to feel her emotions. She went to the stove, put a frying pan on it, and waited as it heated up. Cutting off pieces of bacon, she threw them into the pan, hoping that Kane would choke on the breakfast she was making him. That would serve him right.

She cut off pieces of bread and buttered them, putting them on a baking sheet and sliding them into the oven, getting angrier and angrier each time she felt a twinge of soreness float through her. She was putting herself in physical pain for him and his daughter, and he couldn't even be appreciative of all she was doing? Yes, choking sounded like a fitting punishment.

When he walked through the kitchen to get the milk and eggs, she refused to even look at him. His handsome face didn't even begin to make up for his terrible attitude. She understood that he was still hurting from the death of his wife, but to treat her like she was second class? That was unacceptable from that moment going forward. No longer would she put up with it. She didn't want little Ruth to learn that it was all right for a husband to disrespect his wife.

Berniece took up the bacon and poured a mixture of milk and eggs into the pan, cooking the scrambled eggs in the bacon grease. Just as Kane stomped back into the house, she put his food on a plate and pulled the toast from the oven, slapping that on there as well.

"Coffee?" she asked, hearing the harshness of her own voice.

"Yes." No "please." No "thank you." Just "yes." The man needed to learn some manners, and she was just the woman to teach him.

She poured him a cup of coffee and then got her own plate ready. Truly, he was driving her absolutely crazy, and he'd only said one word to her all morning. She sat down and took a bite of her bacon, spotting an eggshell in the eggs. She knew she should apologize, but she was beyond that. She couldn't even speak to the man without exploding at the moment.

Kane looked at his wife warily, wondering what bee was in her bonnet. He'd thought they'd mended things between them the night before, and here she was, angry with him for *something,* and he didn't even know what it could be. He poked his eggs with his fork and saw an eggshell. Her cooking the day before had been perfect. Had she left shells in on purpose? "There are shells in the eggs."

Berniece closed her eyes and counted to ten. "But there's no poison in them, so you should be thanking me."

His eyes widened. "You're thinking about poisoning me?" Why on earth would she be angry with him? He'd apologized for his bad behavior, and he was treating her well.

"It's what you deserve! Do you have any idea how many hours I spent yesterday putting this house to rights? My entire body aches from all I did, and you never even once said thank you, and instead you complained that I had someone here helping me. I don't know what your problem is, but I will not be your whipping girl. I'm here to be a mother to your daughter and to take care of your house and your meals. I don't even get a real marriage out of it. I'm more or less an unpaid servant in this home. And you can't even thank me for the work I do *without pay?* I will not put up with that type of behavior any longer!" Berniece was shaking with anger by the time she finished her tirade, and she took a sip of milk to cool herself off.

"I apologized to you for my assumptions. What more do you want from me?" Kane felt his own temper rising to meet hers. She was being absolutely unreasonable.

"I want thanks for all I do. Thanks for taking care of your child and cleaning and cooking. Thanks for working so hard to make you happy." Berniece chomped on a bite of her bacon. "And I want you to stop glaring at me as if you think I'm here trying to usurp your precious Veronica."

Veronica's name felt like a slap in the face to Kane. "It's not like you're not getting anything out of this arrangement. Remember that man your parents wanted you to marry? He's not beating on you, and you never have to look at him again. You're doing what you would have done married to him, but you're doing it without being hurt!"

"And that should make me content, should it? I am doing everything I came here to do, and I feel like I've done it all with a good attitude. But I'm sick and tired of you not even thanking me for working so hard and cleaning up the mess of almost a year. I deserve that, not just the cold shoulder, which is all I get from you!" The last words were almost a scream, and in response, she heard a cry from upstairs. "Now look what you did. You woke the baby!" She got up and hurried up the stairs to take care of Ruth, leaving him sitting there, picking the shells out of his eggs.

By the time she had changed the baby and dressed her for the day, Kane was gone. She wanted to scream at him some more, but she knew it wasn't a good idea with the baby watching. The child needed to feel like she lived in a home with love in the air, whether she did or not.

She fed the baby and washed the dishes before sweeping the kitchen floor. She was actually relieved that Kane left before she got back down, because she couldn't keep badgering him about his behavior, no matter how much she wanted to.

Making a pot of chicken, vegetable, and barley soup was easy enough, and they would have it for lunch. She could even feed some bites of it to the baby. She felt like she was constantly thinking about the best things to feed the baby, because Ruth had to be her focus.

She thought for a moment about doing the rest of the laundry, but her arms needed the rest. She would do it all on Monday, and that would become her routine. Laundry every Monday. She'd already looked at the basement and found there was a spot to hang a clothesline there for snowy or rainy days. She was a little surprised not to find one there already.

She baked a couple of fresh loaves of bread for the day, and she planned to serve one with the soup for lunch. Then she sat on the sofa in the parlor, with the baby lying on a quilt on the floor, and she worked on mending the clothes that Kane had thrown into a basket to be dealt with later. She couldn't believe how many things were there that needed to be worked on, but she started on one thing on the top of the heap. If she could mend one item per day and keep up with the baby and other household chores, she would consider it good.

The baby gurgled happily while Berniece sewed, and she was thrilled that Ruth was such a good baby. If she had been a fussy baby, she wasn't sure how she would have handled it.

When it was time for lunch, she served two bowls of the soup and cut up some of the bread, adding a small ball of butter. She would need to make butter as soon as her arms were recovered enough from all the other work she'd done.

Berniece looked up when Kane came in the door at five after twelve. She had a bowl of soup in front of her that she hadn't yet touched, and she was feeding the baby small bites out of another bowl.

Kane sat down at the end of the table and bowed his head to say grace. He frowned down at the soup. "I prefer something heartier than soup for lunch with as hard as I work."

Berniece glared at him. "I think you'll find that my soup is very hearty." She couldn't believe after their talk that morning he was still being rude.

He took a bite of the soup, blowing on it first. He was surprised by all of the chicken, vegetables, and barley in the soup. "I guess it's not too bad."

"Not too bad? Is that how you compliment someone's cooking?" she asked. He could easily have said something kinder, but he was too sure of himself to bother.

He shrugged. "I guess I don't think you need to be complimented for doing your *job*." His slight emphasis on the word *job* had her ready to start screaming all over again.

Berniece bit her lip to keep from saying what she really wanted to, but she knew yelling at him with the baby present was not something she wanted to start now, because she wasn't sure she could go back. Instead, she started to plan her escape for the afternoon.

As soon as he was gone, she put the last of the soup into the ice box, and she cleaned the kitchen. She knew she'd be coming back, and she wasn't about to return to the filth she'd had when she arrived two days prior.

Once the kitchen was clean, she went upstairs and packed enough things for her and Ruth to stay a couple of nights with Charlie and Abel. She had to get away from the man, so he could appreciate all she'd done. She put the clothes they needed in the empty space at Ruth's feet in her buggy, and then she added some clothes that needed to be mended. She couldn't sit around idly while she was in town, no matter how much she wanted to or how much Kane thought that was her desire.

She scrawled a quick note to him.

Kane,

Ruth and I will be in town for a couple of nights. There are plenty of leftovers in the ice box for you to eat. When you're ready to be appreciative of all I do, please come and fetch us from your brother's house.

Berniece

Walking to town was actually very nice for her. The cool September breeze and the beauty of the area she lived in made her feel so much better about how things were going. It was good to be able to walk and let her thoughts flow freely from one topic to the next. Her and Ruth leaving for a while would be a wake-up call that Kane dearly needed, and hopefully he would understand where she was coming from.

When she reached Charlie's house, her friend was there with a wide grin. "I'm so glad you came to visit!"

Berniece stepped inside, pushing the baby's buggy into the entryway. "I'm hoping we can stay for a night or two. Kane and I have had a couple of run-ins today, and I think he needs to be taught how to treat a lady."

"I think you're exactly right. I heard how he talked to you yesterday, and I was appalled." Charlie looked down into the buggy at the sleeping child and smiled widely. "I'm so glad you brought the baby. You have no idea how much I've been missing having her here. I keep listening for her cry, and it never comes, because she doesn't' live here anymore." Charlie shook her head.

"I brought mending to do so I wouldn't just be sitting idle. And I'm happy to help you with supper or anything you need. I'm not trying to get out of working, but I am trying to get away from the constant arguing." Berniece didn't think her new friend shared her husband's views of her, but she had to make sure.

"Of course." Charlie made a face. "I hate mending, so I have a nice little pile myself. Why don't we sit together and work?"

"That sounds lovely. I love little Ruth, but she isn't the best conversationalist while I'm working on something." Berniece had taken to singing while she worked, because the baby reacted well to it.

Charlie grinned. "Yeah, until she starts talking, work will be a little lonely. But then, if she's like my younger siblings, once she starts talking, you'll want her to stop. Quickly."

Berniece laughed. "I have no younger siblings, so I'm unaware of feeling that way. I hope Ruth won't always be an only child." She bit her lip after that. She didn't know if Charlie knew that she and Kane hadn't consummated their marriage and probably never would.

Charlie shook her head. "Kane is going to come around, you know. He's a good man, but he got a raw deal with Veronica. He just needs to see that you're not like her, and everything will be better."

"Wait . . . what? I thought Veronica was this paragon of female virtues. He won't even talk about her, and that makes me feel like she was so perfect, he can't deal with a day without her."

"Not at all. I shouldn't have said as much as I did, and I'm not going to say more, but . . . Kane needs to tell you all of it when he's ready. Just keep being kind to him, and things will look up."

Berniece frowned, looking at her hands. "I guess leaving shells in his eggs and yelling at him like a shrew this morning didn't help anything."

Charlie threw back her head and laughed. "Maybe it will wake him up and cause him to see you for you and not taint you with the memories of other women." The way she emphasized "other women" had Berniece grinning.

"I guess I need to be more patient with him and stop being a brat. I just . . . I wish he appreciated something I did. Anything I did. He never once thanked me for all the work I've done since I arrived, and I ache from it. He did apologize last night for being rude to me about you being there, though. That helped a little."

"But he needs to be grateful as well. I think you letting him know what you need in a husband can only be a good thing."

"I hope so." Ruth made a noise, and Berniece gathered her up immediately. "Oh no! I forgot her bottles and infant food."

Charlie smiled. "I kept some here. I knew you'd be visiting, and it will be easier than taking everything back and forth."

"You know . . . I may not have the best marriage right now, but marrying Kane gave me the mother-lode of sisters-in-law. I'm grateful to you and the help you are to me and little Ruth. Thank you for being you."

"Happy to do it. And honestly, I'm sure you and Kane are going to be happy. It's just a matter of you working together to get through this rough time at the beginning. You're going to make things work. I just know it. You're the sister-in-law I need as well." With those words, Charlie went into the kitchen to make a bottle for the baby, while Berniece looked down into her big blue eyes.

"Are you hungry? Auntie Charlie is making you some milk. Do you want to eat?"

Ruth gurgled something completely incomprehensible to Berniece, and Berniece smiled. "That's right. You just keep talking to me, and

I'll figure it out soon enough. I'm so happy to be your new mommy, Ruthie. I can't believe just how happy your little smile makes me." As happy as she was unhappy with Ruth's father. Hopefully soon, the two would meet in the middle and all would be right with the world. She hoped.

When Charlie came back with the bottle, she scooped the baby up. "I get to feed her. You feed her all the time now." Charlie sat back down and saw to the baby's feeding, while Berniece picked her mending back up.

"I know you. You're trying to keep from having to do the mending."

Charlie nodded emphatically. "You've figured me out."

Berniece grinned as she applied herself to the mending that still needed to be done. She would try and help Charlie with any mending that she needed to do now that she knew how much the other woman hated it. It would be a break for her to go over and let Charlie take care of Ruth while she did her mending for her. Berniece truly didn't mind the task, and she would be happy to help someone who had only shown her love and kindness.

As Charlie became involved with the baby, Berniece's mind went back over everything they'd said that day about Veronica and Kane. Hopefully she could get Kane to understand that she was a hard worker and she only wanted to be a good wife to him. If she worked at it enough, he'd start believing her. He had to.

Chapter Six

WHEN KANE ARRIVED HOME after work, he found his home empty and nothing cooking on the stove. He was still frustrated from the way his wife had acted that day, and he wanted her to be there so he could yell at her. He found a note from Berniece on the table and read it quickly, throwing it down.

He heated up some of the soup she'd made—which was very hearty and exactly what he needed for a good meal—while he thought about what he wanted to do about the situation. As he ate three bowls of the delicious soup he'd criticized just a few hours before, he became angrier and angrier. How dare Berniece take his daughter and run off to town with her? Charlie and Abel had no right to keep the two of them from him. They were his family.

As soon as he'd finished his third bowl of the soup, he put the pot back in the ice box with the same towel she'd draped over it. He thought about leaving the dishes, but with all the work she'd gotten done in the house already, he felt like that would be a slap in the face. Instead, he washed out his bowl, his spoon, and the glass he'd had milk from and wiped them dry. And then he headed into town. He had something to say to his brother and sister-in-law.

He drove into town in the wagon, fully expecting to collect his wife and child while he was there and bring them back to the ranch where they belonged. When he walked into his brother's house, he could hear laughter coming from the parlor. Female laughter. Apparently Berniece wasn't as upset as she'd made it seem earlier.

When he stepped into the parlor, he glared. "Get Ruth and your things. I'm taking you home."

Berniece simply stared at him. "As soon as I feel welcome and as if it *is* my home, I'll consider it." She felt brave with Charlie beside her and Abel sitting in a chair in the same room. Ruth was already asleep for the night.

"Abel, tell her she's leaving with me," Kane said, disbelieving his own eyes and ears. His wife was refusing to go home with him in front of other people. He had no idea what her problem was, but he wasn't pleased. At all.

Abel slowly shook his head. "From what she and Charlie have told me, you don't deserve to have someone as nice as her as your wife. You need to remember how to speak to a woman with respect."

"Are you kidding me?" Kane was shaking with anger. His own brother was taking his wife's side against him? That wasn't right!

Charlie got to her feet and walked to him. "I'd like to speak with you alone for a moment, Kane. I hope you can spare me a few minutes." Her voice was soft and sweet, as it usually was, but he saw a hardness in her eyes that had him backing up a step.

"Yes, ma'am. I think I could spare a moment or two."

"Come into my office," she said, grasping his upper arm and dragging him toward the kitchen.

He grinned. Dragging might be a bit of an exaggeration. It was more of her tugging at him and him following along so his brother wouldn't clobber him later. Abel was older than he was, and he'd always been able to kick his butt. He didn't need to experience that in front of their wives, though.

Once they were in the kitchen, Charlie let go of his arm and turned on him, her eyes full of fire. "Do you know anything at all about your wife? Do you have any idea how hard she's worked since she's arrived in Montana, all to try to make you happy and your surroundings habitable?"

Kane shrugged. "She knew what she was getting into when she married me. My letter was very specific about what I needed from her."

Charlie took a step closer to him, poking him in the middle of his chest with her pointy little finger. For such a delicate woman, he was surprised at just how savage her poke was. "She didn't expect to spend her entire life paying for Veronica's sins, though, did she? She thinks you all but worshipped Veronica. You need to tell her about Ruth's mother, and you need to do it soon. And you need to start thanking her for the things she does for you. I'm tired of seeing her being treated like an indentured servant instead of like the lady she is!"

Kane folded his arms across his chest, trying to look tough but mostly trying to protect his chest from her vicious little finger. "What? I should be thanking her for doing her job?"

"Yes, you should. You should be thanking her every time she puts a meal on the table in front of you. Every time you have something clean to wear and something clean to eat from. Every time you don't have to change a diaper. Berniece is the best thing that has ever happened to you and that baby, and if you continue to treat her poorly, I will do everything I can to help her get an annulment and find a man who will provide well for her—and for Ruth."

"You wouldn't!"

"Oh, I definitely would. I've watched how you've treated her for too long. An hour was too long! And now it's time for you to court your wife. She is staying here until she chooses to return to the ranch. Period. You may call on her after church tomorrow and perhaps take her for a drive or a picnic or maybe even both. But you will not tell her what her duty is or take her for granted. Do you understand me?" Charlie was on tiptoe by the end of her little speech, trying to make herself taller so she could scold him without feeling small. At least that's why he thought she was doing it.

He shook his head. "You seriously think I need to woo my wife?"

She nodded emphatically. "Yes, I do. I think you need to treat her like she's the most beautiful woman you've ever laid eyes on. Treat her like you would have treated a beautiful woman who moved to town before you ever met Veronica." She sighed. "I know you got a raw deal with your first wife. I knew that the moment I met her. But I also know that Berniece is absolutely *nothing* like Veronica. You need to give her a chance to show you how good a marriage can be. Do you know she's worried that you'll never come around and Ruth will be an only child like she was? She wants children. And my baby needs more cousins."

Kane closed his eyes for a moment as he thought about what she'd said. "All right. I'll do the right thing."

"And the right thing is?" Charlie obviously didn't trust him to do what she'd told him. She needed him to spell out his plan for her.

"I will go in the parlor right now and ask her if she will take a drive with me tomorrow and perhaps fix a picnic lunch for us to share." He frowned. "Will you watch Ruth if she agrees?"

"I will be happy to watch Ruth. You know that. I love that little girl as if she was my own."

"All right. I'll go ask her now, but if she says no, I'm not sure what I'll do." He walked toward the parlor, feeling rather than seeing Charlie right on his heels. When he was in the parlor facing Berniece, he took his hat off and held it over his heart, as he'd been taught to do in polite company. "Berniece, would you be willing to accompany me on a drive tomorrow?"

Berniece wanted to scream no at him, but Charlie was standing behind him nodding emphatically. She didn't have the option of saying no apparently. "Yes, I will do that. After church?"

"Yes, after church. And if you would like, I'd be happy to stop for a picnic along the way. I'm afraid you'll have to fix the picnic, though, because I'm not much for cooking." It felt strange to Kane to ask to court his wife, but it felt right as well. Berniece was special, and Charlie was right. He hadn't given her a chance to prove herself. Instead, he'd assumed she was just like Veronica, and that wasn't fair to anyone.

After a moment, Berniece nodded. "I can do that. I'm not sure about taking the baby out, though. The winds have been high lately . . ."

"Charlie has already agreed to watch Ruth for us while we're gone." He took a step toward her. "I want you to know that I appreciate all the work you've done since you came to Montana, and I'm sorry that I haven't treated you better. I hope you're willing to start with a fresh slate tomorrow."

"Yes, I think starting fresh would be good for both of us."

"Will you walk me to the door?" he asked, not sure why. He knew it would make Charlie happy, but more than that, it would make *him* happy.

Berniece set whatever she'd been sewing—one of his shirts, it looked like—aside and followed him to the front door. "Was there something else you wanted to say?" she asked him.

He shook his head. "No, but I wanted to let you know I'm not just apologizing because Charlie is making me. Maybe that's a small part of it, but I really am sorry for treating you so poorly since you arrived. Will you forgive me?"

She nodded, a slow smile on her face. "Yes, I will. Besides, we're starting with a clean slate tomorrow, so no apologies are necessary."

He grinned at that, leaning down and kissing her cheek. "I'll see you at church in the morning, and I'd be honored if you and Ruth would sit by me."

Berniece nodded. "I'd be happy to." And she would. She would have Charlie to introduce her to the other women, and she would feel like she belonged as she sat holding Ruth beside him.

"I appreciate it."

With those words, he left, and Berniece stood staring at the closed door behind him, a smile on her face. Maybe he was a good man after all.

She returned to the parlor, a silly grin on her face, and she sat down on the sofa, picking up the shirt she'd been mending. As she worked on it, she was aware of Charlie and Abel watching her, but she said nothing. They didn't need to know what she was thinking about anyway.

BERNIECE WOKE EARLY to get the picnic ready for lunch and get Ruth ready for church. She put a beautiful gown on the baby, and it occurred to her someone had worked hard sewing for Ruth. She would need to take over that task as soon as she was caught up on everything else.

When she got to church with Charlie and Abel, Kane was waiting beside his wagon, and he immediately offered her his arm. They walked into the church like a perfectly happy newlywed couple. It occurred to her that he probably wanted people to think they were doing well and had never argued, so she made a point of looking at him with a smile. She caught other women smiling at them as they headed to the pew they would share with Charlie and Abel.

As soon as they were seated, Charlie began introducing Berniece to the people who came along. "This is my new sister-in-law. She came here to marry Kane." Charlie didn't add that she was a mail-order bride, which helped Berniece a bit. She didn't want the whole town to know her business anyway. It was enough that Charlie and Abel knew she and Kane had been fighting.

As she met more and more women, Berniece began to feel a little overwhelmed. She'd only ever really attended the church that she'd grown up going to, so there were few strangers. This was a church entirely populated by strangers.

As soon as everyone took their seats to begin the service, Berniece sighed with relief. "So glad that's over."

Charlie laughed. "Most of the women in town are nice, but I don't really know many of them. Once Veronica died, it was easier to stick to myself and just spend time with MaryAnn and the baby."

Kane returned to sit beside Berniece, and he smiled at her tentatively, as if he was still a little worried she'd be angry with him.

"Clean slate, remember?" she whispered to him, and he grinned, nodding.

"Clean slate. I couldn't ask for a better gift from my beautiful bride."

Berniece blushed, having never been given a genuine compliment by a man before. It felt strange.

After the service, they hurried out of the church, and Charlie took Ruth. "We'll take care of her. You two go have fun."

Berniece nodded, smiling. "We won't be too terribly long." Though she wanted to be. This Kane seemed so different than the one she'd been getting to know since she arrived in Missoula. He helped her into the wagon and made sure she was comfortable before walking around and picking up the leads.

"I thought a nice drive out of town would be good. We'll find a good spot for a picnic. How would you feel about eating beside the river?" he asked.

"There's a river? I know so little about this place. I've only been to the mercantile, the train station, the church, and Charlie's house. Everything else is a mystery to me."

"Well, then I need to show you around the whole area. I hope you feel like a long drive." He smiled over at her, and she grinned back. The picnic basket was stowed in the back, and she gripped his arm as he drove. She could feel the ripples of muscles under it, and it caused a small flutter in her belly.

He drove in a full circle around the city, stopping at the Bitterroot River. "We can picnic here." He pulled a quilt from the back and put the picnic basket in her hands. "I'll spread the quilt."

She nodded, smiling at him. She'd had no idea her husband could be quite so charming. He'd kept up a steady stream of conversation on the drive, pointing out different sights and answering her questions. It was so much more pleasant than she'd imagined spending time with him could be.

Once they were seated, she pulled out two ears of corn and the fried chicken she'd made for them. "It won't be hot now, but it should still be good."

"I'm sure it's fine." He reached into the picnic basket for one of the jars of water she'd added in, and he unscrewed the lid, tilting his head back and drinking. A lone trickle of water rolled down the length of his throat, and all she could think about was licking it off his skin.

She blinked a couple of times, forcing herself to look away. She wasn't even sure where that thought had come from. Keeping her eyes on the chicken, she took a bite and smiled. Even though it wasn't hot, it was still warm, and the food was good.

They ate through everything she'd brought, including a dozen chocolate chip cookies, mostly in silence. She desperately wanted to ask him about Veronica after what Charlie had said the previous day, but she wasn't sure how he'd react.

Finally, she found her courage and looked at him. "Tell me about your first marriage."

He frowned, looking down at his hands for a moment. "I'm not quite ready to talk about Veronica yet."

"All right." She looked away, wishing he wasn't keeping secrets from her. Veronica's name had been mentioned a couple of times at church, and she felt as if the whole town knew some sort of secret that she could only guess at.

He reached over and covered her hand with his. "I'm sorry. I'm not trying to hide anything from you, but I'm just not ready to discuss her. I know that's strange."

She simply nodded, wishing things were different between them and she could get him to tell her whatever everyone else knew. He moved toward her on the quilt, looking deeply into her eyes. "I really am sorry."

She shrugged. "I guess if you can't talk about it, then you can't. Maybe someday." She thought for a moment about asking around town, but if he didn't want her to know about Veronica, then she would wait until he did. Yes, there were ways of figuring things out, but at that moment, she knew it was more important for her to trust him. She leaned forward and rested her forehead against his shoulder. "When you are ready to talk, I'll be here."

He pressed a kiss to the top of her head, finding affection with her a great deal easier than he'd expected. She felt right to him in a way that Veronica never had. He rested his cheek atop her head for a moment when something caught his eye. "Stay very still," he said softly, reaching for the gun he always wore at his hip. He knew some said you shouldn't wear a gun to church, but he couldn't *not* wear one. It frightened him just thinking about it.

Berniece moved closer to him, nervous about what must be behind her for him to act so peculiarly. She was afraid, plain and simple.

He pulled the gun and fired two shots. The first went into the rattlesnake's head, and the second cut it in half. When she turned and saw the dead snake, she gasped, shaking her head and throwing herself into his arms.

Chapter Seven

KANE WRAPPED HIS ARMS around his wife, holding her close. He found himself thankful for the snake, because it had made Berniece move closer to him. He looked down at her, tilting her chin up to his, not surprised when he saw tears on her cheeks. "It's okay."

She took deep, gulping breaths before nodding. "Thank you for saving me."

"Happy to do it. Especially since it brought you so close." He wiggled his eyebrows a little to make her laugh, which she did.

"I think I'm done sitting on the ground for our picnic for the moment."

"I can understand that. Do you want to drive for a little more, or should I get you back to Abel's house?"

Berniece looked up at him, pursing her lips as she considered the question. "Why don't we get Ruth from Abel's and go home?" Because suddenly, it did feel like home. There were still secrets between them, but they would be taken care of when the time was right. At least after this sweet time together, she had a hope that the time would eventually be right, and she wouldn't need to continue worrying about her future.

He smiled and nodded. "I'd like that a lot. And I'm not going to take you and all you do for me for granted anymore. I promise you that."

"Thank you." Berniece didn't feel the need to say anything else on the subject. They had a clean slate. "Let's go get our baby girl."

Kane grinned. "I think you already do think of her as yours, don't you?"

She nodded emphatically. "I do. I came here to be her mommy, and that's what I intend to be."

"So, you're what? A mail-order mommy?"

"Well, I'm certainly not much of a mail-order bride. We do keep separate bedrooms after all." She got to her feet and started to clear away the remains of their picnic, putting the refuse and dirty dishes into the basket. She would make sure she cleaned them for Charlie before they went home to the ranch.

"Do you want to share a room?" he asked, looking perplexed. "I honestly thought I was doing you a favor by not sharing a room with you."

"For now, I think it's good. I would like more children eventually, though. Little Ruth doesn't need to be an only child forever."

He stood up and folded the quilt they'd used for the picnic. "Then let's plan on sharing a room whenever you're ready."

Berniece carried the basket and the sloppily folded quilt to put them into the back of the wagon. "I thought you found me repulsive," she said, not meeting his eyes.

"Repulsive? Why would you even think that?" Kane caught her shoulders before she could run over and get into the wagon. "I think you're one of the prettiest women I've ever met."

"Then why did you only kiss my cheek at the wedding? I thought for sure we'd kiss our first time after we were pronounced man and wife, but instead, you just kissed my cheek. It made me feel . . . ugly."

He shook his head, feeling like the world's biggest heel. "I'm so sorry. I didn't intend to have a real marriage with you, and I was planning on treating you like a maid. Which I did for a day or two, if you'll recall. I didn't kiss you, because you shouldn't kiss your maid." He looked deeply into her eyes for a moment. "Are you sure you want to be a wife and not a hired servant?"

Berniece nodded emphatically. "I'm positive."

Kane needed no further invitation. He pulled her to him by the hands that were still gripping her shoulders and lowered his mouth to hers. The kiss he gave her was soft and tentative. This woman was nothing like Veronica, and she deserved to be treated well.

Berniece wrapped her arms around his shoulders, surprising herself. She was actually enjoying this kiss, when she'd loathed every kiss she'd received before. She moved closer to him, flattening her breasts against the hard wall of his chest and opening her mouth for him. Together, they held one another and explored, forgetting the past few days of frustration with each other and only thinking about how the other felt against them.

Kane lifted his head after a long moment. "I think I like kissing you, Mrs. Burton."

She smiled, resting her forehead against his shoulder. "I know I like being kissed by you, Mr. Burton."

He took her hand and pulled her to the side of the wagon, taking her by the waist and easily lifting her into the wagon. "Let's go get our baby so we can go home."

"I'd like nothing more," she said, her eyes full of warmth. She wanted to spend the rest of the day with him, but at their home and not out where they could be stumbled upon by anyone. She liked the intimacy of kissing him, and she didn't want to become a public spectacle.

When they arrived to pick up Ruth, she was sleeping, so Berniece took care of the picnic basket, returning it in perfect condition. She waited until Kane had gone off to speak with Abel before refolding the quilt properly and giving it to Charlie.

"I couldn't let you take it back with the way it was so sloppily folded," she whispered.

Charlie laughed. "Kane must have helped."

"He did. In his own special way."

Charlie grinned. "He's been a good brother to me. I shouldn't poke fun."

"Today was lovely. We went for a long drive, and then we had a picnic. He shot a rattlesnake that was inches from me, and that was fun . . ." Berniece gave a little shudder as she told her friend what had happened.

"He what? It didn't get you, did it?" Charlie looked at her friend as if she was trying to spot a snake bite.

"No, I'm fine, but I was a little *rattled.*"

Charlie laughed appropriately. "I can't believe you're making jokes about it so soon. I think it would take me a great deal longer to get over my initial shock."

"Oh, trust me. I'm still shaking a little." Berniece shook her head. "I feel like Kane and I are getting stronger together. This was a good move for me, though I wasn't sure how it would turn out."

"I think you did what you needed to do. If he starts taking you for granted now, he's never going to stop." Charlie shook her head. "You are definitely doing the right thing for your future as his wife."

Charlie brought Ruth down the stairs a few minutes later, handing her off to her father. The baby looked at her father and patted his cheek happily. It was obvious they had truly bonded during the time they'd had to live apart.

On the drive home, Berniece held the baby, who babbled constantly and incoherently. "She's in a good mood," Berniece said with a grin.

Kane laughed. "I'm not sure I've ever heard her be quite so verbal unless she was crying. I like it."

"I do, too." Berniece kissed the top of the baby's head. "I can't wait until she really starts talking."

"I can't either. I'm told we'll want her to be quiet as soon as she can speak, but I'm not sure I believe that." Kane glanced over at his new wife, holding his daughter, and he felt his heart swell. It truly didn't matter if he thought she was the most beautiful woman on earth. What mattered most to him was how she treated Ruth, and she had already claimed Ruth as her own child. He couldn't have been happier with his choice of brides at that moment. And soon they would learn about each other in a more intimate way. For now, they could simply learn to talk to one another about anything and everything as a way to become closer. "Do you have any siblings?"

Berniece was surprised by the question, but she immediately shook her head. "No, I don't."

"I'm sorry to hear that. I'd have had a horrible time this past year if not for my brother. It wasn't easy even with my brother and his wife's help."

She nodded. "I think I would love to have a sibling. My parents' marriage always felt strange to me, with my mother afraid to contradict my father in any way. I think I understand now. More than I ever dreamed I would understand." Albert Chase had taught her a great deal more than she wanted to know about the negative side of some marriages, and they hadn't even made it to the altar.

"In what way?" Kane knew so little about the woman sitting beside him. The more he learned, the better he felt like they would do together.

"Well, my father bragged to Mr. Chase—the man I was supposed to marry—about how much fun it had been teaching my mother her place early in marriage. And then he went on to say that he still spanked her from time to time so she would remember, not because she needed it any longer." She shook her head. "I cannot believe my mother would stay with a man who treated her that way. And I was appalled she wouldn't help me to avoid a marriage like hers. She honestly thought that's how a marriage should be for some absurd reason."

"I promise you I will never treat you like that. Why did your father want you to marry a man who would beat you?"

"My father thinks women have a weaker mind and must be disciplined. Mr. Chase has been his boss for as long as I can remember, and when he expressed an interest in me, Father knew that he would not spare the rod. That pleased him."

"That's terrible." Kane shook his head. "I'm so thankful I didn't grow up in a household like that." He glanced at the baby, who was still babbling happily. "And I cannot imagine marrying a woman who would hit my child. I want to protect her from everything."

Berniece looked down at little Ruth and nodded. "I want to keep her safe. From the first moment I saw her, I knew it was my job and my responsibility to make sure she never courted a man like Albert Chase."

"What did you like to do back in Beckham?" he asked.

She shrugged. "I volunteered in our local orphanage before I was engaged. I liked that a great deal. I had a few friends who I liked to sit and chat with, but they all married and moved on. I guess I was kind of waiting for my life to start. Oh, and I like to read. A lot. I would read every book I could get my hands on, from poetry to novels to medical treatises. I just like to read."

"I didn't know that!" Kane smiled to himself. He would find her a book or two to commemorate their marriage. Who said he had to wait a year to celebrate anything?

"Yes, what about you? What do you like to do when you have a little spare time?"

He laughed ruefully. "I haven't had any spare time in a long while. When I was married to Veronica, we had to go to town for supper every night, because she didn't cook. So, I'd work all day, and then we'd walk into town, and by the time we got home from supper, it was time for bed. On Sundays we'd stay in town all day so we could go out after church and still be there for supper. And then after Ruth was born, I was spending every moment I had with her. Someday I'll remember what I like to do when I have some spare time, but it won't be soon."

"Can you hire another man to help out around the ranch?" she asked.

He shook his head. "I've hired a lot of extra men, and I find that I just work more to manage them all. No, I need to just take Sundays as relaxation days now. And I have evenings again because you're cooking and not making me go all the way into town." He shrugged. "Trust me, you being here is more help to me than I could possibly express."

"I'm really glad. I read your letter as a cry for help. And it was."

Kane sighed. "I didn't want to be so transparent, but yes, it was. I needed the baby to live with me. I've been taking advantage of Abel and Charlie for too long. And I was afraid her first word would be 'dada' and she'd be talking about Abel, not me. It would have broken my heart into a million tiny little pieces."

"I'm sure it would have." She hugged the baby to her. "I hope her first word is 'mama,' and she means me! Or 'mommy.' That would make me even happier."

"You want to be called Mommy?" he asked.

She nodded. "I think so. I called my mother Mama, but I feel a little betrayed by her. I know she's in a tough situation, but I won't do that to our Ruth, even if I'm in a tough situation. I would take a hundred beatings before I'd let someone lay one finger on her." Her heart was already overflowing with love for little Ruth.

"Thank you," he said softly, surprising her.

"Thanks for what?" she asked. She hadn't expected the words from him at that moment, and she wasn't at all certain what he was referring to.

"Thank you for taking one look at my little girl and making her your own. I don't think I realized just what I had in you until today. Don't change, please." He felt a flash of guilt for the way he'd spoken to her, but he could do nothing other than apologize, and he'd done that. He would do better in future.

Berniece smiled at that. "I'll do my very best."

Once they were home, she set about fixing supper, and then joined Kane and Ruth in the parlor, where they were playing together. She carried the only book she'd had room for on the train, and she opened it up to read it for the thirtieth time. The train ride had been long, and she was a particularly fast reader.

"Have you read that book before?" he asked.

She nodded. "It was the only book I had on the train."

He handed her the baby and left the room for a moment, coming back with three books. "Now these are all I have at the moment, but I'm a particular fan of poetry. Maybe you could read some of them aloud while I hold the baby?"

She grinned. "I would enjoy that more than words can express." She flipped open the book of verses and started on the first. She read aloud, thoroughly excited to share her love of literature with her new family. She wanted little Ruth to be a reader and would start teaching her as soon as she felt the little girl was ready.

More than two hours went by with her reading, and she finally stopped and cleared her throat loudly. "I am going to completely lose my voice if I keep going. Maybe after supper, you could read some?"

"I would enjoy that."

As they ate, Berniece kept stealing looks at him in between taking bites and feeding the baby. For the first time since she'd met him, she was hopeful for the future. She was going to fall in love with him. She could feel it.

Chapter Eight

FOR THE NEXT WEEK, Berniece spent her days alone with little Ruth and her evenings with her new husband. She and Kane were getting more and more comfortable with each other. Berniece completely caught up on the laundry and had moved on to scrubbing the walls and floors upstairs. On Saturday, she made the butter she'd been promising herself she'd make, and her arms were aching when Kane got home that evening.

She had made a pot roast, mashed potatoes, and carrots, along with freshly buttered bread. Kane walked in the door and inhaled deeply before going to the basin to wash his hands. "You are spoiling me, Berniece. I might just start expecting you to do nice things for me." He grinned at her, letting her know he was only half-serious.

She laughed, shaking her head. "A woman cooking dinner for her husband is not spoiling. It's her doing her job."

He frowned. "I'm sorry I ever treated you that way. I don't think it's your job, but I'm so happy you do it willingly." Ruth was in her high chair, and as soon as his hands were washed, he lifted her out. "How was your day? Did your new mommy treat you well?"

Ruth babbled in response and did it very animatedly.

"I think she's just days from crawling," Berniece said. "She was on her hands and knees rocking back and forth as if she was trying to figure out exactly how to do it. Of course, Charlie thought she was really close to crawling for a full month before I got here."

He grinned down at Ruth. "Are you trying to crawl? Now don't you do it for the first time while Daddy is working. I need to *see* you crawl!"

Ruth responded by patting his cheek.

"I think that is meant condescendingly," Berniece said. "It was very much a 'you'll take what you can get' pat."

"I'm worried you're right," Kane said, shaking his head. "I do want her to crawl when I'm around, but I know there will be things I miss unless I stop working, and that wouldn't be smart."

"I'll do my best to write down the time of every new thing and describe it as well as I can. It's as close as I can get to actually being there for you. I wish I was a photographer."

He grinned. "I wish you were, too. I have a feeling that Ruth would find it impossible to stay still for long enough to have her portrait taken. Maybe in a year or two."

Berniece put supper on the table, including freshly cut bread. "Would you mind giving her the heel of the loaf so she can start gnawing on it and we can actually eat a few bites before she starts demanding real food?"

He laughed. "I can do that." He put the baby into her high chair and handed her the heel, watching as she started sucking on it greedily. "I like being able to help out with her a little. Do you know that until MaryAnn and Charlie started trying her on infant food, I'd never even been able to feed her? I've never diapered her. Maybe you could teach me."

She nodded. "I'd be happy to. I wouldn't mind a break from the diapers on occasion. They are not my favorite part of being a mommy, I must say."

"I'm sure they're not, and if I can help with them, I will. I was so excited to have a child, and I feel like I've gotten so little time with her since she was born. You're making it a lot easier for me."

"I'm happy to do that." She took her seat and bowed her head for their prayer, and then she served them both a plate. She took a bit of the carrots and mashed them the best she could with her fork, and then stirred in the mashed potatoes for the baby, setting the bowl aside for the food to cool, while she ate a few bites and the baby gnawed at her bread.

As they ate, Kane told her about the new area they were moving the herd to. "We finally finished mending the fences near the river, so we're moving the herd down that way on Monday. It's going to be a long process, and all of us will have to work together, but I think we can get it done in a day or two."

"I would love to see the whole ranch. Do you know I've lived here for more than a week and never seen the property?"

He shook his head. "I've been remiss. Perhaps we can convince Charlie to watch Ruth tomorrow after church, and the two of us can explore the ranch together."

"I'd like that. Will you have to go on a cattle drive?" she asked, having read about ranches in the west. She'd read about everything.

"I won't go this year, and I didn't last year. When Veronica was pregnant, she wanted me around, and I won't leave my new wife and baby for that long. My ranch foreman will be the one to lead the cattle drive into Billings, which will leave me here with just a couple of hands for a few weeks, but we can get the work done with fewer cattle."

"Will there be someone left to cook for the men? Or should I plan on having a couple of extra mouths to feed every night? It wouldn't be any extra trouble to make more."

He shook his head. "The men that are left will take care of themselves. There's a bunkhouse, and they will take turns making bad food for each other."

She laughed. "Works for me. I can also cook extra, and you can take it to them. Then they won't have to eat their bad food."

"I don't think so. There are times when a man doesn't want his employees close to his beautiful wife." Until he was sure of how she felt about him, he wanted to lock her up and not let her be around other men at all. How had he ever thought this could be a business arrangement?

Beautiful? Berniece felt her heart skip a beat. He was a sweet talker now that he'd decided to be kind, and she wasn't always sure how to take his words. "If you change your mind, let me know, and I'm happy to help out."

"I will." He thought about how Veronica would have yelled at him if he'd even considered asking her to help out by cooking for the ranch hands, and he was happy that he'd found someone as willing to help out as Berniece was. She was a much better wife to him already than Veronica ever had been.

"I'm sorry, but I didn't get around to making a dessert today like I'd planned," she said, shaking her head. "I made butter instead, and my arms are just aching from all the churning. I'm sure I'll get used to it in time, but for now, I don't ever want to even think about lifting a finger ever again."

He laughed. "I'll help with dishes tonight."

"Oh, no. I couldn't ask you to do that!"

"You didn't ask. I offered."

She shook her head. "No, you spent all day working so I can buy food from the store. It's my job to cook that food and clean up after we've eaten it. You play with Ruth, and I'll give her a bath once I've finished with the dishes."

"May I help bathe her? I've never been around for that."

"Of course!" She grinned at him. "I'm just going to bathe her in the basin I wash dishes in. I love our bathtub, but she's still too little to sit up, and it wouldn't be wise to bathe her in it."

Kane smiled. "How do you know so much about children?"

"I volunteered at our local orphanage from the time I graduated from the eighth grade. I helped give the children baths and even got to teach a few of them to read. I changed a lot of diapers there, too. It was a really good experience for me, and I was devastated when my father made me stop helping out." She fed the baby another bite of the mashed-up carrots and potatoes, giggling at the way she opened her mouth like a baby bird, waiting for a worm. "She loves this!"

"She does. She recognizes exceptional cooking already."

Berniece was surprised at the absolute change Kane had made in the week since she'd left overnight. It really had been the right thing to do for their marriage. "I'm glad you enjoy my cooking, but carrots and mashed potatoes are very simple. I did some of that for the orphans as well. And laundry. I think I did more laundry there than anything else!"

"Did your parents encourage you to volunteer? Or was it something you wanted to do?" It sounded like she'd done all the household chores by choice that Veronica had considered beneath her. The more he learned about his sweet new wife, the more he realized he had found someone who was just like he'd thought Veronica was when he married her.

"My mother didn't mind, but my father kept telling me I should be spending my days looking for a husband. I felt like I was too young to look for a husband, and my mother indulged me."

"I don't think that's indulging. That's being reasonable. A woman is not ready to marry until she's a little older."

Berniece smiled and nodded. "I'm nineteen, in case you were wondering, and I think that's a good age for marriage."

"I'm twenty-six," he said softly. "I feel like I'm an old man compared to you."

"How old was Veronica?" she asked casually, hoping he would tell her something about the other woman. What she'd heard so far had made her think Veronica hadn't been a good wife to him, and he was expecting her to act the same.

"She was twenty-one, which is older than you, but she was spoiled and had never worked a day in her life." Kane regretted the words as soon as they were spoken.

"I see." Berniece didn't meet his eyes. "Well, you don't have to worry about that with me. My father called me spoiled, but I certainly know how to work, and I'd rather be busy than idle. Well, unless I have a new book, in which case I can be positively lazy."

He laughed. "I think if you weren't lazy with a new book, you wouldn't be human." He was glad she hadn't latched onto what he'd said about Veronica and had quickly changed the topic. He didn't feel like he should be saying bad things about his late wife, but the truth was, he'd been miserable as soon as they'd said, "I do."

"I'm so glad you understand." She grinned at him as she fed the baby the last of the food she'd made for her. "If you'll watch Ruth, I'll get the dishes done and then draw her bath for her."

"Happy to do it." He'd had three plates of food in the time it had taken Berniece to eat one herself and feed the baby. He scooped the baby out of the chair and wandered into the parlor with her, putting her on her tummy. He wanted to see if she'd crawl for him so he wouldn't miss it while he was working. "Crawl, Ruth!"

Berniece laughed to herself in the kitchen as she heard him tell the baby to crawl. She knew he desperately wanted to have a bigger part in his little girl's life, and she daydreamed about how he would be with their children. Of course, they hadn't yet done anything to make a baby, but they were growing closer, and she was hopeful. Ruth really didn't need to spend her entire life as an only child as Berniece had.

She washed and dried the dishes quickly while she heated water for the baby's bath. When she had the water just right, she called for Kane to bring Ruth in.

"Did she crawl for you?" Berniece asked him.

He shook his head with a frown. "I think she's deliberately holding back so I won't see it."

Berniece laughed. "You are being downright silly, Kane. She doesn't know to do that to you."

He shrugged. "Hopefully she'll crawl for me tomorrow. Then I'll feel like I've seen one of her firsts."

"You'll see plenty of them. Don't worry about that." Berniece took the baby from him and stripped her quickly, putting her in the water and holding her up with a hand behind her head. She picked up a piece of mild soap she'd purchased from the mercantile in town and rubbed it over the baby, carefully washing her hair. When she was done with actually cleaning her, she stepped to one side, while still holding the baby's head up. "Now you can hold her head while she splashes."

Kane put his hand just where Berniece had hers, and then he watched as Ruth kicked and giggled. "She likes the water."

She nodded. "She really does. I forgot to get her diaper and gown. I'll be right back." She hurried up the stairs and carried down one of the baby's long white gowns that had been trimmed with lace. She had made a couple of rompers for the baby that week, so when she was crawling her clothing would be ready. She loved the new style that babies in the East were put into, and whether it was common there in the West or not she didn't know. But her baby would be dressed in the style of the East, and no one could challenge her about it.

When she got back downstairs with the clothes, she stood for a moment at the foot of the stairs, watching Kane with the baby. He was so kind and gentle, and his hands were loving. His voice was low as he talked to the little girl, telling her that she wasn't allowed to even *look* at boys until she was fifty.

Berniece laughed softly as she stepped into the room. "Are you not going to allow her to go to school?"

He turned to her with a grin. "I guess you heard that, huh?"

"I did. Fifty?"

He shrugged. "Maybe forty. I'll see how it goes when I get there." He lifted the baby from the water and handed her to his wife, who waited with a towel.

Drying her off completely, Berniece laid her on the table and diapered her, and then put her in her gown. "Are you ready for sleep, precious?" she asked softly. "We have church tomorrow, so it will be a busy day, and we get to see your auntie Charlie. Yes, we do. She's going to be so happy to get to hold you. We'll have to choose a day next week to go see her, too. I can do her mending, and she can hold you."

"Why would you do Charlie's mending?" Kane asked with surprise.

Berniece shrugged. "She hates mending, and I don't mind it, so I figured she could play with the baby, and I would do her mending. It's more of an excuse to spend a day with her. I've caught up on things around here, and other than making new clothes for the baby, there's not a lot for me to do." She frowned. "I don't want you to think I'm just wasting time . . ."

"I don't." Kane shook his head. "I know what this house would look like if you were just wasting time. You do a good job with Ruth, and you feed me constantly. The house is always immaculate. I think you've earned a couple days a week with Charlie."

"Oh, good. I know that's been a sore spot in the past, and I don't want you to think I would ever not work hard. I just . . . don't feel the need to scrub the floors every day. Once a week is enough."

He smiled. "Once a week is more than enough. There's no need for you to do it more than that." He eyed the baby, who was now fully dressed for bed. "You'll give her a bottle and then put her in her crib?"

Berniece nodded. "That's the nighttime ritual she had at Charlie's, and I've kept it going here. She seems soothed by it."

"Let me give her the bottle, then. Is it ready?"

"Yes, I'll get it for you." She liked taking care of the bedtime routine herself, but she understood how much he would want to take care of his daughter when he could. She gave him the bottle and walked into the parlor with them. "Would you like me to read another poem or two while you feed her?"

He nodded. "That would be wonderful if you really don't mind."

"Not at all." As she read, she watched him with the baby, always impressed by how good he was with her. He put her on his shoulder and burped her when she needed it, and then fed her a bit more.

Finally, the baby fell asleep with the bottle still in her mouth, and he carefully took it out. "I'm going to put her in her crib."

Berniece nodded, reading the next poem as he left the room with the baby.

When he came back a couple of minutes later, he sat down beside her and took the book from her, careful to mark its page with the piece of paper she had there, and then he closed it and put it on an end table. Taking both of her hands in his, he squeezed them. "I think you're right."

She frowned. "I am? That's good to know. About what?"

"I think we should have another baby. I think Ruth needs brothers and sisters, and I know I would love to have another child. What do you think?" he asked.

She stared at him for a moment, surprised that he would say something like that so abruptly. They hadn't even kissed but once. "I think it's definitely a part of our marriage I would like to explore," she said softly.

"Good." He pulled her to him and kissed her slowly and passionately.

She was surprised that he was wanting to start the next baby so soon, but his kisses were intoxicating, and after a moment or two, she couldn't think at all.

He raised his head, breathing heavily. "Are you sure this is what you want?"

She closed her eyes and took a deep breath. Now that she could think again, she knew it wasn't the right time. "I need to know about Veronica first."

He sighed. "I was afraid you'd feel that way. Soon." With that, he got up and walked away from her. She did need to know, but he wasn't sure how to tell her everything. It would happen though. It had to.

Chapter Nine

AFTER CHURCH THE FOLLOWING morning, the two couples went out to lunch with the baby. It was Berniece's first time to eat out since moving to Montana, and she was uncertain how she felt about it.

"We don't have to spend money," she whispered to Kane. "I'm happy to invite everyone to our place, and I'll cook."

He laughed softly. "That's a good idea for next time, but we can afford to eat out on occasion. Don't worry so much. I think you need a break occasionally just like I do."

She was a little relieved that he had decided she'd worked enough to deserve a break. "And after lunch you're going to show me the ranch?" she asked. She wanted time to talk to Charlie first and tell her she needed to know all there was to know about Veronica.

"Yes, if you still want to."

"I do. I want to help Charlie with something first, and then we can go. Oh, and I suppose we should ask her to take care of Ruth."

He laughed. "We shouldn't take her for granted, should we?"

Berniece looked at the woman next to her, who was watching her curiously. "I'm going to show you how to do that thing after lunch, and then we were hoping you'd watch the baby."

Charlie looked at her with a confused expression. "Of course. And I can't wait to learn how to do the thing!" She obviously had no idea what Berniece was talking about, and she shouldn't because there was no thing to show her. She just needed to talk to her.

The café was small, but it was obviously busy. When the waitress came over, she smiled. "I haven't seen you folks for a while. Been busy?"

Charlie nodded. "Well, Berniece came in from Massachusetts to marry Kane, and now we don't need to really eat out much. The men were kind enough to give us a break by bringing us out to eat this afternoon."

"Sundays are good days to take breaks from cooking." The waitress held her notebook. "Water? Coffee? Tea?"

"Water for me," Berniece said.

The waitress wrote all their orders down. "Specials for everyone?" When the other three nodded, Berniece nodded as well.

As the waitress walked away, Berniece asked, "What's the special?"

"Chicken and dumplings today," Kane said. "Whatever the special is, it's always the best food of the day, so that's what we always get."

"I think you've eaten here a lot."

Charlie sighed. "Before I came here, they ate out every single evening, and twice on Sunday. Not even joking."

"That's really sad," Berniece said, shaking her head. She didn't even want to think of all the money they'd wasted.

Abel shrugged. "I can cook a few simple things, but I don't like to eat what I've cooked. Before Charlie came, I was a starving bachelor!"

Berniece raised an eyebrow. "Starving? Really?"

"I might be exaggerating, but just a little bit," he said with a wink.

She shook her head, laughing. "Well, I'm glad that no one eats here for every meal anymore." Looking at Charlie she asked, "How's the morning sickness? Is it getting any better?"

"Yes, finally. I thought I would spend the rest of my life with my head in a chamber pot. Thankfully, I can now eat breakfast again. Usually."

Berniece smiled. "I'm glad you're feeling better. And I appreciate you being willing to watch Ruth this afternoon. Would you believe the only part of the ranch I've seen is the house? Kane is going to show me around today, and we thought it would be best to do it without the baby."

Charlie nodded. "Are you walking or going by horseback?"

"No idea." Berniece looked at Kane. "Do you have an answer to that?"

Kane smiled. "We'll go on horseback. The ranch is much too big to do on foot. Not in one day at least. We could take four or five, but we'd miss the baby."

"Sounds good . . ." She bit her lip. "My father believed that women shouldn't ride horseback, even with a side saddle. I'm not sure we can do this. I've never been on a horse."

Kane shrugged. "We'll ride double, and you can cling to my manly chest and find yourself overrun with passion."

Berniece turned beet red, and her jaw dropped. "Kane Burton! You cannot talk that way in front of other people."

Charlie waved away her objection. "We're not other people. We're family. Besides, Abel would talk that way in front of other people if he thought I'd let him get away with it."

Their water was brought over then, along with a couple of crackers for the baby. Ruth took them greedily, trying to shove a whole cracker in her mouth.

Berniece shook her head and took the crackers away patiently. "That's too much, Ruth. You're going to choke." She broke them into smaller pieces and put just two pieces in front of the little girl, keeping the rest out of her reach. "You'd think she hadn't eaten in a month."

"She's always been a hungry baby," Charlie said, her eyes going soft as she talked about the baby, whom she obviously loved.

"I almost feel bad for taking her away from you," Berniece said. "I can see how much you care about her."

"She's having her own," Abel said softly. "And it's not like she never gets to see little Ruth. You bring her by often."

"Oh, that reminds me. How would you feel if I brought Ruth over on Tuesday afternoon and I did some of your mending while you played with the baby? It would be something of a break for me, because it would be different work, and you wouldn't have to do your own mending."

Charlie grinned. "I can only agree with that if you will allow me to fix supper for you to take home. Then Kane will be fed a good meal even though his wife is off working for no pay for his sister-in-law."

Berniece made a face. "You don't have to do that. I can put a roast in the oven before I leave."

"I won't take no for an answer," Charlie said adamantly.

"Then I guess you're fixing our supper on Tuesday night."

Kane smiled at the arrangement. He liked that the two women got along so well and were so willing to do things for one another. It was another thing that was different about Berniece and Veronica, but there were so many, he just needed to stop comparing them.

When they returned to Charlie and Abel's house after lunch, Berniece took Charlie into the kitchen and sat down at the table with her.

"I don't know what thing you're going to show me," Charlie said, "but I have a feeling what you really wanted was a private talk."

"That's exactly what I want." Berniece lowered her voice to a mere whisper. "I want to know everything you know about Kane's marriage with Veronica. He's ready to be . . . intimate, and I don't want to take that step before I know exactly what he's hiding from me about his first wife."

Charlie shook her head. "I would tell you if I felt like I could, but I fear I've already said too much. You need to get Kane to open up about her."

"It seems too painful for him. Every time I try, he just closes up. He wanted to . . . well, he wanted to last night, but I told him I needed to know about Veronica first, and he went to bed alone rather than talk to me about her. Why won't he open up?"

"You're doing the right thing by making him wait until he can talk about it, but I promise, what he's hiding is not intense feelings for

Veronica. She was . . . well, I've said too much already. You need to talk to him and get him to say whatever he needs to say."

Berniece sighed, leaning back in her chair. "I feel like the entire town is in on a secret that I know nothing about. It's time for someone to break the vow of silence."

"That someone really does need to be Kane and not me. I'm so sorry. I'd tell you anything else."

"I know you would. All right. I'll try to talk to him again today. We'll have plenty of time alone together."

"Good." Charlie got to her feet. "Would you care to stay for supper tonight? Since you'll be out all day exploring, it might be nice to just know it's taken care of."

Berniece pursed her lips as she thought about it. "Only if you'll come to my house for supper on Saturday night. I'll cook a feast."

"I'll bring a pie! The apples are ripe, and it's the perfect time to bake an apple pie."

"Do you want to know something, Charlie?"

"Sure! I like to know things!"

"I think you're one of my favorite people in the world, and I'm sad I didn't know you when we were both growing up in Beckham."

Charlie laughed. "Have you heard the stories about the demon horde that plagued the country school outside of Beckham?"

"Oh, yes!" Berniece shook her head. "There was a big family, and all of the children were monsters. I hear there are still a few that are causing mischief now."

"I'm one of the original demon horde members. Still wish we'd been friends?"

Berniece laughed after a moment of shock. "Yes, I still do. I think your antics would have been fun to watch."

"I'm not so sure . . ."

Kane poked his head into the kitchen then. "Are you ladies finished with your private talk?"

Charlie laughed. "There's no pulling the wool over your eyes, Kane. Yes, we're finished. Take her away. Supper is here at six sharp. That way you can spend all day exploring, and your sweet wife won't have to worry about feeding you."

"You sure you don't mind?" Kane asked.

"Not at all. And we're coming to your house on Saturday for supper, so don't think it's wrong of you to let me cook. Berniece is cooking for us in return."

Kane smiled. "You know too well how I think." He reached for Berniece's hand. "Let's go see my ranch. I think you're going to be amazed by our operation."

"Well, now you have me confused, Kane. Is it yours or ours?" Berniece grinned at him saucily.

"It's ours. Now, hush, and I'll tell you about it as we drive."

On the way, he talked about the size of his ranch and how many head of cattle he ran. He had twenty-five men working for him, and only three were staying behind to help him during the cattle drive that was starting on Monday.

"How many cows are you selling?"

He grinned. "I'm selling *all* the steers and keeping just two bulls. And I'm keeping *most* of the cows. I need them for breeding next year."

"That makes sense. I had no idea you had so many men working for you. Do you enjoy managing men?" she asked.

He shrugged. "Sometimes I do, and sometimes I don't. Last year I had a couple of men who were competing for the same woman's affections. Everything they did was a contest to see who was better, and it made me just a little bit crazy. I felt like I spent more time keeping the two of them from killing each other and outdoing each other than I did working."

"And I'm sure it was hard when Veronica died. Did you have to take much time off work?"

He took a deep breath. "I don't want to talk to you about Veronica, but after talking to Abel today, I can see that I need to. Why don't we go home and talk about everything you need to know, and then if we still have time before supper, I'll show you around the ranch. If we don't, we can do it next week. Snow's going to start soon, but you're a Massachusetts girl, and I would think you can withstand a little cold."

She smiled. "I probably can. I've been known *not* to freeze into a solid block of ice when winter came around."

He grinned at her, but his mind was on the conversation they were about to have, a topic he'd hoped to never have to speak about with his new wife. She had to know, though. He would try really hard to keep her from paying for Veronica's sins in his mind, but she'd already suffered more than she should have to. It was time she knew why.

When they got to the ranch, she went inside and made a pot of coffee while he unhitched the wagon. He spent a good ten minutes talking to his dog, Clyde, trying to explain to him why this was so difficult for him, but Clyde just looked at him as if he'd lost his mind. He was on his own in that arena.

Walking outside the stable, he spotted some late-blooming flowers that he couldn't give the name of if his life depended on it. He picked a small bouquet and took it inside to his wife. While she put the flowers in water and fussed a little, he drank coffee, trying to get up the courage to say what he needed to say to her. How did you tell a woman that he had been a terrible husband to his first wife, but she'd been an even worse wife? He wasn't sure it was possible to do it without losing his mind.

Berniece sat down across from Kane at the table and waited for him to speak for more than a minute. Finally, she decided it was her job to start the conversation. "So, I've gleaned a bit of information from things people have told me. Veronica didn't cook at all. And she didn't particularly care for cleaning either. I'm under the impression she expected everyone around her to do the things a wife should do while she sat back and watched. And then she died in childbirth, and everyone rallied around you to help the baby, but I can't even imagine what your emotions must have been like. Did you love her so much you just couldn't stand it?"

Kane grinned a little and shook his head. "I'm going to have to start at the beginning, and this isn't a short story. But you need to know how it all came about."

"I think I do need to know, and I'm sorry I'm making you talk about such a difficult thing." She reached over and took his hand, squeezing it in her own.

He took a deep breath and started talking, watching her carefully for any adverse reactions. The story was a difficult one.

Chapter Ten

BERNIECE WAS SO HAPPY Kane was finally willing to talk about Veronica she couldn't express it. She was determined to let him say what he needed to say, and she would simply listen to him. It didn't take her long to get angry as he told his story.

"Veronica lived in a small town near here, and her father was a banker. When he lost all his money, he gave her a piece of jewelry to sell, and she was on her own from that day forward. That wasn't Veronica's fault, of course, but it was how everything started. She moved into the hotel here in Missoula, and she set her sights on the richest man in town. When he made it clear he wasn't interested, she moved on to Abel."

"Abel? I had no idea there was ever a courtship between Veronica and Abel."

Kane nodded, moving on. "Abel was flattered that a woman so beautiful was interested in him." He stood up and walked over to a portrait of the baby, and he reached behind it in the frame, pulling out a picture of a beautiful woman. She had blond hair and looked particularly fetching in the dress she was wearing. Taking it to his wife, he handed it to her. "Veronica had a way of making any man feel twenty feet tall when she turned her gaze on him and acted like she was interested in a relationship."

"And their relationship didn't last?"

He shook his head. "She continually talked to him about marriage, and he finally told her he didn't think they would be compatible. I didn't know he'd told her that, and I'd met her a few times, gone to supper with them, that sort of thing. I found out later that he had thought about hosting a supper party, and he asked her if she would be willing to make the meal. She had laughed in response, telling him that she'd never be willing to do the job of servants, but she would be happy to cling to his arm and play hostess."

Berniece nodded. "I can't see Abel being willing to be put up with someone like that."

"He wasn't. Honestly, if I'd had a chance to talk to him, I wouldn't have been willing either." He shrugged. "I went into town the next morning to get some supplies. At that point, I was eating with my men every night, and I was there getting the food we needed for meals. When I got to the store, I found her there, and she was crying. I didn't know better, so I went over to try to soothe her."

"Well, of course. You knew her, and she was new to town."

"Right. Well, I'd always thought she was beautiful and my brother was the luckiest man in all Montana for having her as his sweetheart. I asked her if she was all right, and she threw herself into my arms. She told me that she and Abel had a fight, because she told him that she had feelings for me, and he had yelled at her. I couldn't picture it, but I knew that if anyone could make him angry, it was her. You either wanted to love her or hate her. She said she had nowhere to go and told me about her father losing all his money."

"So, you asked her to marry you and did it right then before you talked to Abel."

"Am I that transparent?" Kane asked, shaking his head. "I was happy for exactly three hours before I found out how she really was. We went to the church, married, and then I took her out for lunch, and she was so sweet. When I got her home, she took one look around my house and asked me why I expected her to live in filth. Then she asked when I was hiring a maid."

Berniece had the strange desire to laugh at that, but she held it in. She couldn't imagine Kane being married to anyone who wasn't willing to work. "Oh my."

He grinned at her. "I guess that explains why I was so worried you'd end up being a wastrel." He sighed deeply. "We managed to live together for all of a week, when she 'borrowed' some of my money that I had left out for household expenses and went back to the hotel. She stayed there for around a month before she came back to me and informed me she was carrying my child and she didn't want it." He could still see how her face looked as she told him how much she wished she'd never conceived the baby.

Berniece shook her head. "I can't imagine a mother not wanting her own child."

"Of course, you can't. You want another woman's child, and the fact that you didn't give birth to her doesn't bother you even a little bit."

"No, it doesn't." She sighed. "She sounds like someone I would want to slap."

Kane laughed softly. "I *did* want to slap her often. But I never did, and I think I should get some sort of medal for that. Well, I used to think so." He shook his head. "She moved back in with me, and we did our best to make things work, but she was constantly telling me that I couldn't expect her to do any kind of work, because she was expecting. I couldn't ask her to cook or clean or even be kind to people. She was pregnant, and she was always sore and hurting."

Berniece understood the knowing looks she'd gotten around town when people found out she was married to Kane. "I've thought this whole time that you loved her so much you couldn't speak about her."

"I never loved her. I was infatuated by her for a few hours. When she died, I felt terrible, because the baby was mine, and she'd died in childbirth, and I couldn't bring myself to be horribly sad she'd died. The guilt has truly overwhelmed me. She wasn't a pleasant or loving person, but she did give me my child. She gave her life for little Ruth, and I need to always respect her for that."

"Respecting her and mourning her are two very different things. I know that if I had married Albert Chase and he had died a short while later, I would have felt only relief. I *couldn't* have mourned him."

"No, I don't suppose you could have." Kane sat down again, and he grasped her hand. "You don't think less of me?"

She shook her head adamantly. "How could I think less of you for that?"

He pulled her to her feet and walked into the parlor with her. "I want you to tell me exactly what happened with Albert Chase now."

Berniece took a deep breath. "You know most of it. My whole life I was aware of the man, because he came over to dinner often, and he was always looking at me as if I belonged to him. He made me feel extremely uncomfortable. If I knew he was coming for supper, I would do my best to go to a friend's house so I didn't have to see him. Or I'd pretend to be sick and stay in my room without eating."

Kane frowned. "Men shouldn't make girls feel that way."

"No, they shouldn't. I always thought of him as an old man. I guess I really became aware of the fact he was my father's boss when I was about five, and already he made me feel bad about myself. The day I turned nineteen, I went home fully expecting a birthday party. My parents had said they would have a surprise for me when I got home from the orphanage. Instead of a party, he was there. He asked me to be his wife, and I said no. I didn't even have to think about it."

"Of course, you didn't."

She smiled. "My father didn't give me the choice. He grabbed me by the shoulder, took me into his office, and told me in no uncertain terms that since I hadn't found a husband by myself, then he had taken the matter into his own hands, and he'd arranged a marriage for me. I was to go out and tell Mr. Chase that I would marry him and beg his forgiveness for my rudeness."

"Did you?"

"Not immediately. It took some convincing and some threats, but finally I did what he said. I apologized, and Albert laughed as if it was all a big joke. He walked me to the door, and he kissed me. Well, he would have called it a kiss, but I would have called it a molestation of my mouth." She shuddered. "I was told the next morning that I needed to stop going to the orphanage because it was time for me to start planning my wedding. It became my job to shop and plan my wedding. Once every week, Albert would take me out for dinner and kiss me, telling me what my duties would be as his wife."

He shook his head. "He sounds like *such* a pleasant man."

"He was worse than you're imagining. Anyway, a few days before I left, he took me to supper, and I asked him why he didn't want to marry someone closer to his age. He was extremely angry when I said that, and he told me he would punish me. He wasn't sure how, but he would come up with a good way to do it, and he would tell me the next time he saw me. He wouldn't punish me until our wedding night, though, because then I would be his." She shuddered as she told him everything. "He wanted me to know what the punishment was so I could think about it for the two months leading up to our wedding."

"And did you tell your parents?" He was more disgusted by her story than he'd imagined he'd be.

"Actually, when he took me home that night, he told my father he would have to find a way to punish me, and they laughed about it. And then my parents left the room so we could 'spark.' As if I wanted that odious old man touching me. I tried to talk to my mother the next morning, and she wouldn't do anything, so I went for a walk and ended up at the mercantile looking at books, as I always did. There I saw an advertisement I'd seen for years but never even thought about . . . until that moment. And I went and talked to Elizabeth Tandy, Charlie's older sister. Elizabeth listened to my story, and she found a way to get me on a train less than forty-eight hours later."

"I'm glad you had the courage to go to her."

Berniece nodded. "I am, too. All I could think about was getting away from that man. My mother wouldn't help me. My father thought it was a good idea. I had to take matters into my own hands—or in my case, put matters in Elizabeth's hands."

He leaned back on the sofa and wrapped his arm around her. "If I were a writing sort, I would need to write a book about Veronica and Albert and how well they would have done together."

"Oh, that's mean. But yes, that's a book I would read." She looked over at him. "Thank you for telling me all that about Veronica. I can see where it wouldn't be something you want your new wife to know, but . . . I could tell there was something I didn't know every time I met a new person in town."

"Does this mean we can move forward now?" He was afraid to look at her as he asked the question. He wanted a real marriage with her, where she did all the things she'd been doing and she shared his bed. That last part was becoming more important by the day.

"I would like that a lot." Berniece took a deep breath, considering telling him she loved him right then, but she wanted to make a big deal out of it. She would make a special supper, and she'd tell him over dessert—as he was marveling at her cooking prowess.

"Me too." He glanced at a clock on the wall. "We've been talking for a very long time. We need to get back to town for supper and so we can bring our daughter home."

"Yes, we do." She got to her feet and smiled down at him. "I'm so glad we talked about these things. I feel like we *really* can move on now."

"I do, too." He got to his feet and drew her against him, kissing her softly. "Thank you for not thinking less of me."

"Well, you could have thought less of me, too. We'll let bygones be bygones, and we can talk about the people who have been so rude to us if we want to." She rested her forehead against his shoulder. "I feel like a load has been lifted off my shoulders. I'm not sure if it's because you told me about Veronica, or if it's because I told you everything about Albert. Either way, I'm glad we had this talk. But I do want to see the ranch sometime."

He smiled. "I know. You'll get to see the ranch." He walked out to hitch up the team, feeling a lot lighter himself. Berniece was good for him.

AFTER HER LAUNDRY THE following day, Berniece made a special supper for Kane. She wanted to tell him she loved him in the nicest way she could think of. She made steak, baked potatoes, and green beans, knowing that he was particularly fond of steak.

When he came in at the end of the day, he looked as if he'd just combed his hair back and he had more flowers in his hand. "I can't pick them after the snow starts, and it could come any day. Farmer's almanac is calling for an early winter."

She walked to him and stood on tiptoe to kiss him. "Thank you. They're lovely."

While he washed his hands and played with Ruth, she arranged the flowers in a vase and put them beside the other, thinking about how overrun with flowers her house was about to be if he kept this up. "How was your day?"

He rubbed the back of his neck tiredly. "The men are off for the cattle drive, and we moved the rest of the herd down to the river."

"Sounds interesting."

"It wasn't a lot of fun, but little of ranch work is. I do love to be outdoors, and I love the animals. And the money isn't too terribly bad." He smiled at her. "Did she crawl today?"

Berniece laughed, shaking her head. "She neither crawled nor spoke. You're good for another day."

"Glad to hear it!"

She put the food in front of him before sitting down and cutting off a small piece of her potato to cool for Ruth. After the prayer, she mashed it up and mashed a few green beans, mixing them together. "This is going to be nummy!"

Kane didn't think it was possible to love a woman as much as he loved Berniece at that moment. She'd spent the day taking care of his baby, made his favorite meal, cleaned house, and now she was talking to the baby as if she were the most important person in her world. "I love you."

Berniece's head turned toward him, and her eyes grew wide. "Did you just say what I think you said?"

He chuckled. "How could I not love someone who gives so much of herself to everything she does?"

"I made this meal special so I could tell you that I love you while you ate it, and here you are saying it before I even get a chance."

"Do you mean it? You really love me?"

"I really do love you, Kane Burton. And I hope we have many happy years together and a dozen children."

He frowned. "As long as your births are easy with all of them."

She shrugged. "I'm not worried about dying in childbirth. With our modern medicine it's happening less and less."

"All right . . ."

After the baby was in bed, he took her into his arms, looking down into her eyes. "Since we love each other, how about sleeping in my bed tonight? I really kind of expected you to last night, but you went to your old room . . ."

"You didn't *ask* me to sleep with you, so I thought you wanted me in my old room. If you say what's on your mind, we'll communicate a lot more clearly."

He smiled at that. "Berniece, I would really enjoy it if you would move into my room and let me make love to you."

She laughed. "Now *that* was clear. I'd be happy to!"

Epilogue

A YEAR AND A HALF LATER, Berniece was sitting up in bed, sweat still on her forehead as she stared into the eyes of a tiny baby boy. The midwife had just left, and Kane was sitting beside her.

"He's beautiful. And you're still alive!"

"I told you I was going to be fine," she said, shaking her head at him. "Should we bring Ruth in to see the baby?"

He nodded, going to get their little girl, who was in the kitchen with her aunt Charlie baking cookies. Ruth had grown into a beautiful little girl with blond ringlets, looking more like her mother than he'd ever dreamed she would, but her disposition was just like Berniece's. She'd learned a great deal from her step-mother.

When Ruth walked in, her eyes were wide with surprise.

"It's a boy?" she asked. Charlie must have told her.

"Yes, it's a boy. What do you think we should name him?"

Ruth wrinkled her little nose. "George?" she asked. Berniece knew there was a little boy named George at the church she liked to speak with.

"How about if we call him Seth? It's a strong Bible name, and it goes well with Ruth." Berniece looked at Kane for his reaction.

"That sounds good to me. We'll keep on going with the bible names."

"Mommy?" Ruth asked, and Berniece's heart swelled, as it did every time the little girl called her that.

"Yes, Ruth?"

"Love you." Ruth climbed onto the bed beside her and rested her head on her mother's shoulder as she looked down at her little brother.

Berniece looked at her children and then over at her husband, and she knew that her life had never felt so complete. "I love you, too, Ruth. And I love your daddy, and I even love little Seth."

Kane walked over and squatted in front of Berniece, looking at the baby. His whole world was right there in that room with him, and he couldn't be happier.